THE VICISSITUDES OF EVANGELINE

Elinor Glyn

A General Books LLC Publication.

CONTENTS

1

SECTION 1

THE BEGINNING OF
EVANGELINE'S JOURNAL

Branches Park,
November yd, 1904.

I Wonder so much if it is amusing to be an adventuress, because that is evidently
what I shall become now. I read in a book all about it; it is being nice-looking and
having nothing to live on, and getting a pleasant time out of lifeland I intend to do
that! I have certainly nothing to live on, for one cannot count $300 a yearland I am
extremely pretty, and I know it quite well, and how to do my hair, and put on my hats,
and those things, so, of course, I am an adventuress! I was not intended for this *role*lin
fact Mrs. Carruthers adopted me on purpose to leave me her fortune, as at that time
she had quarrelled with her heir, who was bound to get the place. Then she was so
inconsequent as not to make a proper willlthus it is that this creature gets everything,
and I nothing!

I am twenty, and up to the week before last, when Mrs. Carruthers got ill, and died
in one day, I had had a fairly decent time at odd moments when she was in a good
temper.

There is no use pretending even when people are dead, if one is writing down one's real thoughts. I detested Mrs. Carruthers most of the time. A person whom it was impossible to please. She had no idea of justice, or of anything but her own comfort, and what amount of pleasure other people could contribute to her day!

How she came to do anything for me at all was because she had been in love with papa, and when he married poor mammala person of no familyland then died, she offered to take me, and bring me up,just to spite mamma, she has often told me. As I was only four I had no say in the matter, and if mamma liked to give me up that was her affair. Mamma's father was a lord, and her mother I don't know who, and they had not worried to get married, so that is how it is poor mamma came to have no relations. After papa was dead she married an Indian officer, and went off to India, and died too, and I never saw her any morelso there it is, there is not a soul in the world who matters to me, or I to them, so I can't help being an adventuress, and thinking only of myself, can I?

Mrs. Carruthers periodically quarrelled with all the neighbours, so beyond frigid calls now and then in a friendly interval, we never saw them much. Several old, worldly ladies used to come to stay, but I liked none of them, and I have no young friends. When it is getting dark, and I am up here alone, I often wonder what it would be like if I hadlbut I believe I am the kind of cat that would not have got on with them too nicelylso perhaps it is just as well; only to have had a prettylaunt, say, to love one, that might have been nice.

Mrs. Carruthers had no feelings like this. " Stuff and nonsense "l"sentimental rubbish " she would have called them. To get a suitable husband is what she brought me up for, she said, and for the last years had arranged that I should marry her detested heir, Christopher Carruthers, as I should have the money, and he the place.

He is a diplomat, and lives in Paris, and Russia, and amusing places like that, so he does not often come to England. I have never seen him. He is quite oldlover thirtyland has hair turning gray.

Now he is master here, and I must leave lunless he proposes to marry me at our meeting this afternoon, which he probably won't do.

However, there can be no harm in my making myself look as attractive as possible under the circumstances. As I am to be an adventuress, I must do the best I can for myself. Nice feelings are for people who have money to live as they please. If I had ten thousand a year, or even five, I would snap my fingers at all men, and say, " No, I make my life as I choose, and shall cultivate knowledge and books, and indulge in beautiful ideas of honour and exalted sentiments, and perhaps one day succumb to a noble passion." (What grand words the thought even is making me write!!) But as it is, if Mr. Carruthers asks me to marry him, as he has been told to do by his aunt, I shall certainly say yes, and so stay on here, and have a comfortable home. Until I have had this interview it is hardly worth while packing anything.

What a mercy black suits me! My skin is ridiculously whitell shall stick a bunch of violets in my frock, that could not look heartless, I suppose. But if he asks me if I am sad about Mrs. Carruthers' death, I shall not be able to tell a lie.

I am sad, of course, because death is a terrible thing, and to die like that, saying spiteful things to every one, must be horridlbut I can't, I can't regret her! Not a day ever passed that she did not sting some part of me |when I was little, it was not only with her tongue, she used to pinch me, and box my ears until Doctor Garrison said it might make me deaf, and then she stopped, because she saiddeaf people were a bore, and she could not put up with them.

I shall not go on looking back! There are numbers of things that even now make me raging to remember.

] have only been out for a year. Mrs. Car- ruthers got an attack of bronchitis when I was eighteen, just as we were going up to town for the season, and said she did not feel well enough for the fatigues, and *off* we went to Switzerland. And in the autumn we travelled all over the place, and in the winter she coughed and groaned, and the next season would not go up until the last court, so I have only had a month of London. The bronchitis got perfectly well, it was heart-failure that killed her, brought on by an attack of temper because Thomas broke the Carruthers vase.

I shall not write of her death, or the finding of the will, or the surprise that I was left nothing but a thousand pounds, and a diamond ring.

Now that I am an adventuress, instead of an heiress, of what good to chronicle all that! Sufficient to say if Mr. Carruthers does not obey his orders, and offer me his hand this afternoon, I shall have to pack my trunks, and depart' by Saturday|but where to is yet in the lap of the gods!

He is coming by the 3.20 train, and will be in the house before four, an ugly, dull time; one can't offer him tea, and it will be altogether trying and exciting.

He is coming ostensibly to take over his place, I suppose, but in reality it is to look at me, and see if in any way he will be able to persuade himself to carry out his aunt's wishes. I wonder what it will be like to be married to some one you don't know, and don't like? I am not greatly acquainted yet with the ways of men. We have not had any that you could call that here, muchlonly a lot of old wicked sort of things, in the autumn, to shoot the pheasants, and play bridge with Mrs. Carruthers. The marvel to me was how they ever killed anything, such antiques they were! Some Politicians and ex-Ambassadors, and creatures of that sort; and mostly as wickedas could be. They used to come trotting down the passage to the schoolroom, and have tea with Mademoiselle and me on the slightest provocation! and say such things! I am sure lots of what they said meant something else, Mademoiselle used to giggle so. She was rather a good-looking one I had the last four years, but I hated her. There was never anyone young and human who counted.

I did look forward to coming out in London, but, being so late, every one was preoccupied when we got thereland no one got in love with me much. Indeed, we went out very little, a part of the time I had a swollen nose from a tennis ball at Ranelaghland people don't look at girls with swollen noses.

I wonder where I shall go and live! Perhaps in Parislunless, of course, I marry Mr. Car- ruthers,|I don't suppose it is dull being married. In London all the married ones seemed to have a lovely time, and had not to bother with their husbands much.

Mrs. Carruthers always assured me love was a thing of absolutely no consequence in marriage. You were bound to love some one, some time, but the very fact of being chained to him would dispel the feeling. It was a thing to be looked upon like measles, or any other disease, and was better to get it over, and then turn to the solid affairs of life. But how she expected me to get it over when she never arranged for me to see anyone I don't know.

I asked her one day what I should do if I got to like some one after I am married to Mr. Carruthers, and she laughed one of her horrid laughs, and said I should probably do as the rest of the world. And what do they do ?|I wonder?|Well, I suppose I shall find out some day.

Of course there is the possibility that Christopher (do I like the name of Christopher, I wonder?)|-well, that Christopher may not want to follow her will.

He has known about it for years, I suppose, just as I have, but I believe men are queer creatures, and he may take a dislike to me. I am not a type that would please every one. My hair is too red, brilliant dark fiery red like a chestnut when it tumbles out of its shell, only burnished like metal. If I had the usual white eyelashes I should be downright ugly, but, thank goodness! by some freak of nature mine are black and thick, and stick out when you look at me sideways, and I often think when I catch sight of myself in the glass that I am really very pretty|all put together| but, as I said before, not a type to please every one.

A combination I am that Mrs. Carruthers assured me would cause anxieties. " With that mixture, Evangeline," she often said, " you would do well to settle yourself in life as soon as possible. Good girls don't have your colouring." So you see, as I am branded as bad from the beginning, it does not much matter what I do. My eyes are as green as pale emeralds, and long, and not going down at the corners with the Madonna expression of Cicely Parker, the Vicar's daughter. I do not know yet what is being good, or being bad, perhaps I shall find out when I am an adventuress, or married to Mr. Carruthers.

All I know is that I want to *live,* and feel the blood rushing through my veins. I want to do as I please, and not have to be polite when I am burning with rage. I want to be late in the morning if I happen to fancy sleeping, and I want to sit up at night if I don't want to go to bed! So, as you can do what you like when you are married, I really hope Mr. Carruthers will take a fancy to me, and then all will be well! I shall stay upstairs until I hear the carriage-wheels, and leave Mr. Barton|the lawyer|to receive him. Then I shall saunter down nonchalantly while they are in the hall. It will be an effective entrance. My trailing black garments, and the great broad stairs|this is a splendid house|and if he has an eye in his head he must see my foot on each step! Even Mrs. Carruthers said I have the best foot she had ever seen. I am getting quite excited. I shall ring|for Veronique and begin to dress! . . . I shall write more presently.

Thursday evening.

It is evening, and the fire is burning brightly in my sitting-room where I am writing. *My* sitting-room!|did I say? Mr. Carruthers' sitting-room I meant|for it is mine no longer, and on Saturday, the day after to-morrow, I shall have to bid good-bye to it forever.

For yes|I may as well say it at once|the affair did not walk. Mr. Carruthers quietly, but firmly, refused to obey his aunt's will, and thus I am left an old maid!

I must go back to this afternoon to make it clear, and I must say my ears tingle as I think of it.

I rang for Veronique, and put on my new black afternoon frock, which had just been unpacked. I tucked in the violets in a careless way. Saw that my hair was curling as vigorously as usual, and not too rebelliously for a demure appearance, and so, at exactly the right moment, began to descend the stairs.

There was Mr. Carruthers in the hall. A horribly nice-looking, tall man, with a cleanshaven face, and features cut out of stone. Asquare chin, with a nasty twinkle in the corner of his eye. He has a very distinguished look, and that air of never having had to worry for his things to fit, they appear as if they had grown on him. He has a cold, reserved manner, and something commanding and arrogant in it, which makes one want to contradict him at once, but his voice is charming. One of that cultivated, refined kind, that sounds as if he spoke a number of languages, and so does not slur his words. I believe this is diplomatic, for some of the old ambassador people had this sort of voice.

He was standing with his back to the fire, and the light of the big window with the sun getting low was full on his face, so I had a good look at him. I said in the beginning that there was no use pretending when one is writing one's own thoughts for one's own self to read when one is old, and keeping them in a locked- up journal, so I shall always tell the truth here lquite different things to what I should say if I were talking to someone, and describing to them this scene. Then I should say I foundhim utterly unattractive, and in fact, I hardly noticed him! As it was, I noticed him very much, and I have a tiresome inward conviction that he could be very attractive indeed, if he liked.

He looked up, and I came forward with my best demure air, as Mr. Barton nervously introduced us, and we shook hands. I left him to speak first.

" Abominably cold day," he said, carelessly. That was English and promising!

"Yes, indeed," I said. "You have just arrived?"

And so we continued in this banal way, with Mr. Barton twirling his thumbs, and hoping, one could see, that we should soon come to the business of the day; interposing a remark here and there, which added to *the gene* of the situation.

At last Mr. Carruthers said to Mr. Barton that he would go round and see the house; and I said tea would be ready when they got back. And so they started.

My cheeks would burn, and my hands were so cold, it was awkward and annoying, not half the simple affair I had thought it would be upstairs.

When it was quite dark, and the lamps were brought, they came back to the hall, and Mr. Barton, saying he did not want any tea, left us to find papers in the library.

I gave Mr. Carruthers some tea, and asked the usual things about sugar and cream. His eye had almost a look of contempt as he glanced at me, and I felt an angry throb in my throat. When he had finished he got up, and stood before the fire again. Then, deliberately, as a man who has determined to do his duty at any cost, he began to speak:

" You know the wishlor rather, I should say, the command, my aunt left me," he said l" in fact she states that she had always brought you up to the idea. It is rather a tiresome thing to discuss with a stranger, but perhaps we had better get it over as soon as possible, as that is what I came down here to-day for. The command was, I should marry you."|He paused a moment. I remained perfectly still, with my hands idly clasped in my lap, and made myself keep my eyes on his face.

He continued, finding I did not answer| just a faint tone of resentment creeping into his voice|because I would not help him out, I suppose|I should think not! I loved annoying him!

" It is a preposterous idea in these days for any one to dispose of people's destinies in this way, and I am sure you will agree with me that such a marriage would be impossible."

" Of course I agree," I replied, lying with a tone of careless sincerity. I had to control all my real feelings of either anger or pleasure for so long in Mrs. Carruthers' presence that I am now an adept.

" I am so glad you put it so plainly," I went on sweetly. " I was wondering how I should write it to you, but now you are here it is quite easy for us to finish the matter at once. Whatever Mrs. Carruthers may have intended me to do, I had no intention of obeying her, but it would have been useless for me to say so to her, and so I waited until the time for speech should come. Won't you have some more tea?"

He looked at me very straightly, almost angrily, for an instant; presently, with a sigh of relief, he said, half laughing|

" Then we are agreed, we need say no more about it! "

" No more," I answered, and I smiled too, although a rage of anger was clutching my throat. I do not know who I was angry with |Mrs. Carruthers for procuring this situation, Christopher for being insensible to my charms, or myself for ever having contemplated for a second the possibility of his doing otherwise. Why, when one thinks of it calmly, should he want to marry me ? A penniless adventuress with green eyes, and red hair, that he had never seen before in his life. I hoped he thought I was a person of naturally high colour, because my cheeks from the moment I began to dress had been burning and burning. It might have given him the idea the scene was causing me some emotion, and that he should never know!

He took some more tea, but he did not drink it, and by this I guessed that he also was not as calm as he looked!

"There is something else," he said. And now there was almost an awkwardness in his voice. " Something else which I want to say, though perhaps Mr. Barton could say it for me |but which I would rather say straight to you|and that is you must let me settle such a sum of money on you as you had every right to expect from my aunt, after the promises I understand she always made to you "

This time I did not wait for him to finish! I bounded up from my seat|some uncontrollable sensation of wounded pride throbbing and thrilling through me.

"Money!|Money from you!" I exclaimed. 'Not if I were starving! "|then I sat down again, ashamed of this vehemence. How would he interpret it! But it galled me so, and yet I had been ready an hour ago to have accepted him as my husband ! Why, then, this revolt at the idea of receiving a fair substitute in gold ? Really, one is a goose, and I had time to realize, even in this tumult of emotion, that there can be|nothing so inconsistent as the feelings of a girl.

" You must not be foolish!" he said, coldly. "I intend to settle the money whether you will or no, so do not make any further trouble about it! "

There was something in his voice so commanding and arrogant, just as I noticed at first, that every obstinate quality in my nature rose to answer him.

" I do not know anything about the law in the matter; you may settle what you choose, but I shall never touch any of it," I said, as calmly as I could; " so it seems ridiculous to waste the money, does it not ? You may not, perhaps, be aware I have enough of my own, and do not in any way require yours."

He became colder and more exasperated.

" As you please, then," he said, snappishly, and Mr. Barton, fortunately entering at that moment, the conversation was cut short, and I left them.

They are not going back to London until tomorrow morning, and dinner has yet to be got through. Oh! I do feel in a temper, and I can never tell of the emotions that were throbbing through me as I came up the great stairs just now. A sudden awakening to the humiliation of the situation! How had I ever been able to contemplate marrying a man I did not know, just to secure myself a comfortable home! It seems preposterous now. I suppose it was because I have always been brought up to the idea, and until I came face to face with the man, it did not strike me as odd. Fortunately he can never guess that I had been willing to accept him|my dissimulation has stood me in good stead. Now I am animated by only one idea! To appear as agreeable and charming to Mr. Carruthers as possible. The aim and object of my life shall be to make him regret his decision. When I hear him imploring me to marry him, I shall regain a little of my self- respect ! And as for marriage, I shall have nothing to do with the horrid affair! Oh dear no! I shall go away free, and be a happy adventuress |I have read the " Trois Mousquetaires," and " Vingt Ans Apres "|Mademoiselle had them |and I remember milady had only three days to get round her jailer, starting with his hating her, whereas Mr. Carruthers does not hate me, so that counts against my only having one evening. I shall do my best|!

Thursday night.

I Was down in the library, innocently reading a book when Mr. Carruthers came in. He looked even better in evening dress, but he appeared ill-tempered, and no doubt found the situation unpleasant.

" Is not this a beautiful house ? " I said, in a velvet voice, to break the awkward silence, and show him I did not share his unease. " You had not seen it before, for ages, had you ?"

" Not since I was a boy," he answered, trying to be polite. " My aunt quarrelled with my father|she was the direct heiress of all this, and married her cousin, my father's younger brother|but you know the family history, of course "

" Yes."

" They hated one another, she and my father."

" Mrs. Carruthers hated all her relations," I said demurely.

" Myself among them ?"

" Yes," I said slowly, and bent forward, so that the lamplight should fall upon my hair. " She said you were too much like herself in character for you ever to be friends."

"Is that a compliment?" he asked, and there was a twinkle in his eye.

" We must speak no ill of the dead," I said, evasively.

He looked slightly annoyed, as much as these diplomats ever let themselves look anything.

" You are right," he said. " Let her rest in peace."

There was silence for a moment.

" What are you going to do with your life now?" he asked, presently. It was a bald question.

" I shall become an adventuress," I answered deliberately.

" A *what* ?" he exclaimed, his black eyebrows contracting.

"An adventuress. Is not that what it is called ? A person who sees life, and has to do the best she can for herself."

He laughed. " You strange little lady?" he said, his irritation with me melting. And when he laughs you can see how even his teeth are, but the two side ones are sharp and pointed like a wolf's.

" Perhaps after all you had better have married me!"

" No, that would clip my wings," I said frankly, looking at him straight in the face.

" Mr. Barton tells me you propose leaving here on Saturday. I beg you will not do so| please consider it your home for so long as you wish|until you can make some arrangements for yourself. You look so very young to be going about the world alone!
"

He bent down and gazed at me closer| there was an odd tone in his voice.

" I am twenty, and I have been often snubbed," I said, calmly; " that prepares one for a good deal. I shall enjoy doing what I please."

" And what are you going to please ?"

" I shall go to Claridge's until I can look about me."

He moved uneasily.

" But have you no relations ? No one who will take care of you ?"

" I believe none. My mother was nobody particular you know|a Miss Tonkins by name."

" But your father ?" He sat down now on the sofa beside me; there was a puzzled, amused look in his face|perhaps I was amazing him.

" Papa ? Oh ! Papa was the last of his family |they were decent people, but there are no more of them."

He pushed one of the cushions aside.

" It is an impossible position for a girl| completely alone. I cannot allow it. I feel responsible for you. After all, it would do very well if you married me|I am not particularly domestic by nature, and should be very little at home|so you could live here, and have a certain position, and I would come back now and then to see you were getting on all right."

One could not say if he were mocking, or no.

" It is too good of you," I said, without any irony, " but I like freedom, and when you were at home it might be such a bore "

He leant back, and laughed merrily.

" You are candid, at any rate!" he said.

Mr. Barton came into the room at that moment, full of apologies for being late. Immediately after, with the usual ceremony, the butler entered and pompously announced, " Dinner is served, sir." How quickly they recognize the new master!

Mr. Carruthers gave me his arm, and we walked slowly down the picture gallery to the banqueting hall, and there sat down at the small round table in the middle, that always looks like an island in a lake.

I talked nicely at dinner. I was dignified and grave, and quite frank. Mr. Carruthers was not bored. The *chef* had outdone himself, hoping to be kept on. I never felt so excited in my life.

I was apparently asleep under a big lamp, after dinner in the library|a book of silly poetry in my lap|when the door opened and he|Mr. Carruthers|came in alone, and walked up the room. I did not open my eyes. He looked for just a minute|how accurate I am! Then he said, " You are very pretty when asleep!"

His voice was not caressing, or complimentary, merely as if the fact had forced this utterance.

I allowed myself to wake without a start.

" Was the '47 port as good as you hoped ?" I asked, sympathetically

He sat down. I had arranged my chair so that there was none other in its immediate neighbourhood. Thus he was some way off, and could realize my whole silhouette.

" The '47 port|oh yes!|but I am not going to talk of port. I want you to tell me a lot more about yourself, and your plans."

"I have no plans|except to see the world."

He picked up a book, and put it down again§; Jie was not perfectly calm.

" I don't think I shall let you. I am more than ever convinced you ought to have some one to take care of you; you are not of the type that makes it altogether safe to roam about alone."

" Oh! as for my type," I said, languidly, " I know all about that. Mrs. Carruthers said no one with this combination of colour could be good, so I am not going to try. It will be quite simple."

He rose quickly from his chair, and stood in front of the great log fire, such a comical expression on his face.

" You are the quaintest child I have ever met," he said.

" I am not a child|and I mean to know everything I can."

He went over towards the sofa again, and arranged the cushions|great, splendid, fat pillows of old Italian brocade, stiff with gold and silver.

" Come! " he pleaded, " sit here beside me, and let us talk; you are miles away there, and I want to|make you see reason."

I rose at once, and came slowly to where he pointed. I settled myself deliberately, there was one cushion of purple and silver right under the light, and there I rested my head.

" Now talk! " I said, and half closed my eyes.

Oh! I was enjoying myself! The first time I have ever been alone with a real man ! They |the old ambassadors, and politicians, and generals, used always to tell me I should grow into an attractive woman|now I meant to try what I could do.

Mr. Carruthers remained silent|but he sat down beside me, and looked, and looked right into my eyes.

" Now talk then," I said again.

" Do you know, you are a very disturbing person," he said at last, by way of a beginning.

"What is that?" I asked.

" It is a woman who confuses one's thought when one looks at her. I do not now seem to have anything to say|or too much."

" You called me a child."

" I should have called you an enigma."

I assured him I was not the least complex, and that I only wanted everything simple, and to be left in peace, without having to get married, or worry to obey people.

We had a nice talk.

" You won't leave here on Saturday," he said, presently, apropos of nothing. " I do not think I shall go myself, to-morrow. I want you to show me all over the gardens, and your favourite haunts."

"To-morrow I shall be busy packing," I said, gravely, " and I do not think I want to show you the gardens|there are some corners I rather loved|I believe it will hurt a little to say good-bye."

Just then Mr. Barton came into the room, fussy and ill at ease. Mr. Carruthers' face hardened again, and I rose to say good-night.

As he opened the door for me: "Promise you will come down to give me my coffee in the morning," he said.

" *jui vtvra verra"* I answered, and sauntered out into the hall. He followed me, and watched as I went up the staircase.

" Good-night! " I called softly, as I got to the top, and laughed a little|I don't know why.

He bounded up the stairs, three steps at a time, and before I could turn the handle of my door, he stood beside me.

" I do not know what there is about you," he said, "but you drive me mad|I shall insist upon carrying out my aunt's wish after all! I shall marry you, and never let you out of my sight|do you hear ?"

Oh ! such a strange sense of exaltation crept over me|it is with me still! Of course he probably will not mean all that to-morrow, but to have made such a stiff block of stone rush upstairs, and say this much now is perfectly delightful!

I looked at him up from under my eyelashes. " No, you will not marry me," I said, calmly; " or do anything else I don't like, and now really good-night!" and I slipped into my room, and closed the door. I could hear he did not stir for some seconds. Then he went off down the stairs again, and I am alone with my thoughts.

2

SECTION 2

My thoughts! I wonder what they mean. What did I do that had this effect upon him? I intended to do something, and I did it, but I am not quite sure what it was. However, that is of no consequence. Sufficient for me to know that my self-respect is restored, and I can now go out and see the world with a clear conscience.

He has asked me to marry him! and *I* have said I won't!

Branches Park, *Thursday night, Nov. yd,* 1904.

Dear Bos,1lA quaint thing has happened to me! Came down here to take over the place, and to say decidedly I would not marry Miss Travers, and I find her with red hair and a skin like milk, and a pair of green eyes that look at you from a forest of black eyelashes with a thousand unsaid challenges. I should not wonder if I commit some folly. One has readof women like this in the *cinque-cento* time in Italy, but up to now I had never met one. She is not in the room ten minutes before one feels a sense of unrest, and desire for one hardly knows whatlprincipally to touch her, I fancy. Good Lord! what a skin! pure milk and rare rosesland the reddest Cupid's bow of a mouth! You had better come down at once, (these things are probably in your line) to save me from some sheer idiocy. The situation is exceptional; she and I practically alone in the house, for old Barton does not count. She has nowhere to go, and as far as I can make out has not a friend in the world. I suppose I ought to leaveI will try to on Monday, but come down to-morrow by the 4 train.

1 A letter from Mr. Carruthers which came into Evangeline's possession later, and which she put into her journal at this place. (Editor's note.)

Yours,

Christopher.

P.S. '47 port Ai, and two or three brands of the old aunt's champagne exceptional, Barton says; we can sample them. Shall send this up by express, you will get it in time for the 4 train.

Branches,

Friday night, November th.

This morning Mr. Carruthers had his coffee alone. Mr. Barton and I breakfasted quite early, before 9 o'clock, and just as I was calling the dogs in the hall for a run, with my out-door things already on, Mr. Carruthers came down the great stairs with a frown on his face.

" Up so early! " he said. " Are you not going to pour out my tea for me, then ?"

" I thought you said coffee! No, I am going out," and I went on down the corridor, the wolf-hounds following me.

" You are not a kind hostess! " he called after me.

" I am not a hostess at all," I answered back, " only a guest."

He followed me. " Then you are a very casual guest, not consulting the pleasure of your host."

I said nothing; I only looked at him over my shoulder, as I went down the marble stepsI looked at him, and laughed as on the night before.

He turned back into the house without aword, and I did not see him again until just before luncheon.

There is something unpleasant about saying good-bye to a place, and I found I had all sorts of sensations rising in my throat at various points in my walk. However, all that is ridiculous, and must be forgotten. As I was coming round the corner of the terrace, a great gust of wind nearly blew me into Mr. Car- ruthers' arms. Odious weather we are having this autumn.

"Where have you been all the morning?" he said, when we had recovered ourselves a little. " I have searched for you all over the place."

" You do not know it all yet, or you would have found me," I said, pretending to walk on.

" No, you shall not go now," he exclaimed, pacing beside me. " Why won't you be amiable, and make me feel at home."

" I do apologize if I have been unamiable," I said, with great frankness. " Mrs. Carruthers always brought me up to have such good manners."

After that he talked to me for half an hour about the place.

He seemed to have forgotten his vehemence of the night before. He asked all sorts of questions, and showed a sentiment and a delicacy I should not have expected from his hard face. I was quite sorry when the gong sounded for luncheon and we went in.

I have no settled plan in my head|I seem to be drifting,|tasting for the first time some power over another human being. It gave me delicious thrills to see his eagerness when contrasted with the dry refusal of my hand only the day before.

At lunch I addressed myself to Mr. Barton ; he was too flattered at my attention, and continued to chatter garrulously.

The rain came on, and poured, and beat against the window-panes with a sudden angry thud. No chance of further walks abroad. I escaped upstairs while the butler was speaking to Mr. Carruthers, and began helping Veronique to pack. Chaos and desolation it all seemed in my cosy rooms.

While I was on my knees in front of a great wooden box, hopelessly trying to stow away books, a crisp tap came to the door, and without more ado my host|yes, he is that now| entered the room.

" Good Lord! what is all this," he exclaimed, " what are you doing ?"

"Packing," I said, not getting up.

He made an impatient gesture.

" Nonsense! " he said, " there is no need to pack. I tell you I will not let you go. I am going to marry you and keep you here always."

I sat down on the floor and began to laugh.

" You think so, do you ? "

" Yes."

" You can't force me to marry you, you know|can you ? I want to see the world, I don't want any tiresome man bothering after me. If I ever do marry it will be because|

oh, because " and I stopped, and began

fiddling with the cover of a book.

"What?"

" Mrs. Carruthers said it was so foolish|but I believe I should prefer to marry some one I liked. Oh! I know you think that silly," and I stopped him as he was about to speak, "but of course, as it does not last any way, it might be good for a little to begin like that, don't you think so ? "

He looked round the room, and on through the wide open double doors into my dainty bedroom where Veronique was still packing.

" You are very cosy here, it is absurd of you to leave it," he said.

I got up off the floor and went to the window and back. I don't know why I felt moved, a sudden sense of the cosiness came over me. The world looked wet and bleak outside.

" Why do you say you want me to marry you, Mr. Carruthers?" I said. "You are joking, of course."

" I am not joking. I am perfectly serious. I am ready to carry out my aunt's wishes. It can be no new idea to you, and you must have worldly sense enough to realize it would be the best possible solution of your future. I can show you the world, you know."

He appeared to be extraordinarily good- looking as he stood there, his face to the dying light. Supposing I took him at his word, after all.

" But what has suddenly changed your ideas since yesterday ? You told me you had come down to make it clear to me that you could not possibly obey her orders."

"That was yesterday," he said. " I had not really seen you; to-day I think differently."

" It is just because you are sorry for me; I suppose I seem so lonely," I whispered demurely.

" It is perfectly impossible|what you propose to do|to go and live by yourself at a London hotel|the idea drives me mad! "

" It will be delightful! no one to order me about from morning to night! "

" Listen," he said, and he flung himself into an armchair. " You can marry me, and I will take you to Paris, or where you want, and I won't order you about,|only I shall keep the other beasts of men from looking at you."

But I told him at once I thought that would be very dull. " I have never had the chance of any one looking at me," I said, " and I want to feel what it is like. Mrs. Carruthers always assured me I was very pretty, you know, only she said that I was certain to come to a bad end, because of my type, unless I got married at once, and then if my head was screwed on the right way it would not matter; but I don't agree with her."

He walked up and down the room Impatiently.

" That is just it," he said. " I would rather be the first|I would rather you began by me. I am strong enough to ward *off* the rest."

" What does ' beginning by you' mean ?" I asked with great candour. " Old Lord Bent- worth said I should begin by him, when he was here to shoot pheasants last autumn; he said it could not matter, he was so old; but I didn't "

Mr. Carruthers bounded up from his chair.

" You didn't what! Good Lord, what did he want you to do! " he asked aghast.

"Well," I said, and I looked down for a moment, I felt stupidly shy, " he wanted me to kiss him."

Mr. Carruthers appeared almost relieved, it was strange!

" The old wretch ! Nice company my aunt seems to have kept! " he exclaimed. " Could she not take better care of you than that|to let you be insulted by her guests."

" I don't think Lord Bentworth meant to insult me. He only said he had never seen such a red, curly mouth as mine, and as I was bound to go to the devil some day with that, and such hair, I might begin by kissing him| he explained it all."

" And were you not very angry ?" his voice wrathful.

" No|not very, I could not be, I was shaking so with laughter. If you could have seen the silly old thing, like a wizened monkey, with dyed hair and an eyeglass, it was too comic !|I only told you because you said the sentence ' begin by you,' and I wanted to know if it was the same thing."

Mr. Carruthers' eyes had such a strange expression, puzzle and amusement, and something else. He came over close to me.

" Because," I went on, " if so, I believe if that is always the beginning|I don't want any beginnings|I haven't the slightest desire to kiss any one|I should simply hate it."

Mr. Carruthers laughed. " Oh! you are only a baby child after all! " he said.

This annoyed me. I got up with great dignity. " Tea will be ready in the white drawing- room," I said stiffly, and walked towards my bedroom door.

He came after me.

" Send your maid away, and let us have it up here," he said. " I like this room."

But I was not to be appeased thus easily, and deliberately called Veronique and gave her fresh directions.

" Poor old Mr. Barton will be feeling so lonely," I said, as I went out into the passage. " I am going to see that he has a nice tea," and I looked back at Mr. Carruthers over my shoulder. Of course he followed me and we went together down the stairs.

In the hall a footman with a telegram met us. Mr. Carruthers tore it open impatiently. Then he looked quite annoyed.

" I hope you won't mind," he said, " but a friend of mine, Lord Robert Vavasour is arriving this afternoon|he is a|er|great judge of pictures. I forgot I asked him to come down and look at them, it clean went out of my head."

I told him he was host; and why should I object to what guests he had.

" Besides, I am going myself to-morrow," I said," if Veronique can get the packing done."

"Nonsense|how can I make you understand that I do not mean to let you go at all."

I did not answer|only looked at him defiantly.

Mr. Barton was waiting patiently for us in the white drawing-room, and we had not been munching muffins for five minutes when the sound of wheels crunching the gravel of the great sweep|the windows of this room look out that way|interrupted our manufactured conversation.

" This must be Bob arriving," Mr. Carruthers said, and went reluctantly into the hall to meet his guest.

They came back together presently, and he introduced Lord Robert to me. i

I felt at once he was rather a pet! Such a shape! Just like the Apollo of Belvidere! I do love that look, with a tiny waist and nice shoulders, and looking as if he were as lithe as a snake, and yet could break pokers in half like Mr. Rochester in "Jane Eyre! "

He has great, big, sleepy eyes of blue, and rather a plaintive expression, and a little fairish moustache turned up at the corners, and the nicest mouth one ever saw, and when you see him moving, and the back of his head, it makes you think all the time of a beautifully groomed thoroughbred horse. I don't know why. At once|in a minute|when we looked at one another, I felt I should like " Bob "! He has none of Mr. Carruthers' cynical, hard, expression, and I am sure he can't be nearly as old, not more than twenty-seven, or so.

He seemed perfectly at home, sat down and had tea, and talked in the most casual, friendly way. Mr. Carruthers appeared to freeze up, Mr. Barton got more banal|and the whole thing entertained me immensely.

I often used to long for adventures in the old days with Mrs. Carruthers, and here I am really having them!

Such a situation! I am sure people would think it most improper! I alone in the house with these three men! I felt I really would have to go|but where!

Meanwhile I have every intention of amusing myself!

Lord Robert and I seemed to have a hundred things to say to one another. I do like his voice|and he is so perfectly *sans gene,* it makes no difficulties. By the end of tea we were as old friends. Mr. Carruthers got more and more polite, and stiff, and finally jumped up and hurried his guest off to the smoking-room.

I put on such a duck of a frock for dinner, one of the sweetest chastened simplicity, in black, showing peeps of skin through the thin part at the top. Nothing could be more demure or becoming, and my hair would not behave, and stuck out in rebellious waves and curls everywhere.

I thought it would be advisable not to be in too good time, so sauntered down after I knew dinner was announced.

They were bothstandingon the hearth rug. I always forget to count Mr. Barton, he was in some chair, I suppose, but I did not notice him.

Mr. Carruthers is the tallerlabout one inch; he must be a good deal over six feet, because the other one is very tall too, but now that one saw them together Mr. Carruthers' figure appeared stiff and set beside Lord Robert's, and he hasn't got nearly such a little waist. I wonder if any other nation can have that exquisitely *soigne* look of Englishmen in evening dress, I don't believe so. They really are lovely creatures, both of them, and I don't yet know which I like best.

We had such an engaging time at dinner! I was as provoking as I could be in the timel sympathetically absorbingly interested in Mr. Barton's long stories, and only looking at the other two now and then from under my eyelasheslwhile I talked in the best demure fashion that I am sure even Lady Katherine Montgomeriela neighbour of ourslwould have approved of.

They should not be able to say I could not chaperone myself in any situation.

" Dam- good port this, Christopher," Lord Robert said, when the '47 was handed round. " Is this what you asked me down to sample ?"

" I thought it was to give your opinion about the pictures," I exclaimed, surprised. " Mr. Carruthers said you were a great judge."

They looked at one another.

" Ohlahlyes," said Lord Robert, lying transparently. " Pictures are awfully interesting. Will you show me them after dinner ?"

" The light is too dim for a connoisseur to investigate them properly," I said.

" I shall have it all lit by electricity as soon as possible; I wrote about it to-day," Mr. Carruthers announced, sententiously. "But I will show you the pictures myself, to-morrow, Bob."

This at once decided me to take Lord Robert round to-night, and I told him so in a velvet voice while Mr. Barton was engaging Christopher's attention.

They stayed such a long time in the dining- room after I left that I was on my way to bed when they came out into the hall, and could with difficulty be persuaded to remain for a few moments.

" I am too awfully sorry! " Lord Robert said. " I could not get away, I do not know what possessed Christopher, he would sample ports, and talked the hind leg off a donkey, till at last I said to him straight out I wanted to come to you. So here I aml now you won't go to bed, will youlplease, please."

He has such pleading blue eyeslimploring pathetically like a baby in distresslit is quite impossible to resist him ! and we started down the gallery.

Of course he did not know the difference between a Canaletto and a Turner, and hardly made a pretence of being interested, in fact when we got to the end where the earlyItalians hang, and I was explaining the wonderful texture of a Madonna, he said:

" They all look sea-sick, and out of shape! don't you think we might sit in that comfy window seat and talk of something else! " Then he told me he loved pictures, but not this sort.

" I like people to look human you know, even on canvas," he said. " All these ladies appear as if they were getting enteric like people used in Africa, and I don't like their halos, and things, and all the men are old and bald. But you must not think me a Goth|you will teach me their points, won't you, and then I shall love them."

I said I did not care a great deal for them myself, except the colour.

" Oh! I am so glad," he said. " I should like to find we admired the same things; but no picture could interest me as much as your hair. It is the loveliest thing I have ever seen, and you do it so beautifully."

That did please me! He has the most engaging ways, Lord Robert, and he is verywell informed, not stupid a bit, or thick, only absolutely simple and direct. We talked softly together, quite happy for a while.

Then Mr. Carruthers got rid of Mr. Barton, and came towards us. I settled myself more comfortably on the velvet cushions. Purple velvet cushions and curtains in this gallery, good old relics of early Victorian taste. Lots of the house is awful, but these curtains always please me.

Mr. Carruthers' face was as stern as a stone bust of Augustus Caesar. I am sure the monks in the Inquisition looked like that. I do wonder what he meant to say, but Lord Robert did not give him time.

"Do go away, Christopher," he said ; "Miss Travers is going to teach me things about Italian Madonnas, and I can't keep my attention if there is a third person about."

I suppose if Mr. Carruthers had not been a diplomat he would have sworn, but I believe that kind of education makes you able to put your face how you like, so he smiled sweetly, and took a chair near.

" I shall not leave you, Bob," he said. " I do not consider you are a good companion for Miss EVangeline. I am responsible for her, and I am going to take care of her."

" Then you should not have asked him here if he is not a respectable person," I said, innocently; "but Italian Madonnas ought to chasten and elevate his thoughts. Anyway your responsibility towards me is self constituted. I am the only person whom I mean to obey! " and I settled myself deliberately in the velvet pillows.

"Not a good companion ! " exclaimed Lord Robert, " What dam- cheek, Christopher. I have not my equal in the whole Household Cavalry, as you know."

They both laughed, and we continued to talk in a sparring way, Mr. Carruthers sharp, subtle, and fine as a sword blade|Lord Robert downright, simple, with an air of a puzzled baby.

When I thought they were both wanting me very much to stay, I got up, and said goodnight.

They both came down the gallery with me, and insisted upon each lighting a candle from the row of burnished silver candlesticks in the hall, which they presented to me with great mock homage. It annoyed me, I don't know why, and I suddenly froze up, and declined them both, while I said good-night again stiffly, and walked in my most stately manner up the stairs.

I could see Lord Robert's eyebrows puckered into a more plaintive expression than ever, while he let the beautiful silver candlestick hang, dropping the grease on to the polished oak floor.

Mr. Carruthers stood quite still, and put his light back on the table. His face was cynical and rather amused. I can't say what irritation I felt, and immediately decided to leave on the morrow|but where to, Fate, or the Devil, could only know!

When I got to my room a lump came in my throat. Veronique had gone to bed, tired out with her day's packing.

I suddenly felt utterly alone, all the exaltation gone. For the moment I hated the twodownstairs. I felt the situation equivocal, and untenable, and it had amused me so much an hour ago.

It is stupid and silly, and makes one's nose red, but I felt like crying a little before I got into bed.

Branches,

Saturday afternoon, Nov. $t/.

This morning I woke with a headache, to see the rain beating against my windows, and mist and fog|a fitting day for the fifth of November. I would not go down to breakfast. Veronique brought me mine to my sitting-room fire, and, with Spartan determination, I packed steadily all the morning.

About twelve a note came up from Lord Robert; I paste it in :

" Dear Miss Travers,|Why are you hiding? Was I a bore last night? Do forgive me and come down. Has Christopher locked you in your room ? I will murder the brute if he has!

" Yours very sincerely,

" Robert Vavasour."

" Can't, I am packing," I scribbled in pencil on the envelope, and gave it back to Charles, who was waiting in the hall for the answer. Two minutes after Lord Robert walked into the room, the door of which the footman had left open.

" I have come to help you," he said in that voice of his that sounds so sure of a welcome you can't snub him; " but where are you going?"

" I don't know," I said, a little forlornly, and then bent down and vigorously collected photographs.

" Oh, but you can't go to London by yourself! " he said, aghast. " Look here, I will come up with you, and take you to my aunt, Lady Merrenden. She is such a dear, and I am sure when I have told her all about you she will be delighted to take care of you for some days until you can hunt round."

He looked such a boy, and his face was so kind, I was touched.

" Oh no, Lord Robert! I cannot do that, but I thank you. I don't want to be under an obligation to any one," I said firmly. " Mr. Carruthers suggests a way out of the difficulty |that I should marry him, and stay here. I don't think he means it really, but he pretends he does."

He sat down on the edge of a table already laden with books, most of which overbalanced and fell crash on the floor.

" So Christopher wants you to marry him, the old fox! " he said, apparently oblivious of the wreck of literature he had caused. " But you won't do that, will you ? And yet I have no business to say that. He is a dam- good friend, Christopher."

" I am sure you ought not to swear so often, Lord Robert, it shocks me, brought up as I have been," I said, with the air of a little angel.

" Do I swear ? " he asked, surprised. " Oh no, I don't think so|at least there is no ' n ' to the end of the ' dams,' so they are only an innocent ornament to conversation. But I won't do it, if you don't wish me to."

After that he helped me with the books, and was so merry and kind I soon felt cheered up, and by lunch time all were finished, and in the boxes ready to be tied up, and taken away. Veronique, too, had made great progress in the adjoining room, and was standing stiff" and *maussade* by my dressing-table when I came in. She spoke respectfully in French, and asked me if I had made my plans yet, for, as she explained to me, her own position seemed precarious, and yet having been with me for five years, she did not feel she could leave me at a juncture like this. At the same time she hoped Mademoiselle would make some suitable decision, as she feared (respectfully) it was " *une si drole de position pour une demoiselle du monde*" alone with *"ces messieurs."*

I could not be angry, it was quite true what she said.

" I shall go up this evening to Claridge's, Veronique," I assured her, " by about the 5.15 train. We will wire to them after luncheon."

She seemed comforted, but she added, in the abstract, that a rich marriage was what was obviously Mademoiselle's fate, and she felt sure great happiness and many jewels would await Mademoiselle, if Mademoiselle could be persuaded to make up her mind. Nothing is sacred to one's maid ! She knew all about Mr. Carruthers, of course. Poor old Veronique| I have a big, warm corner for her in my heart |sometimes she treats me with the frigid respect one would pay to a queen, and at others I am almost her *enfant,* so tender and motherly she is to me. And she puts up with all my tempers and moods, and pets me like a baby just when I am the worst of all.

Lord Robert had left me reluctantly when the luncheon gong sounded.

" Haven't we been happy ?" he said, taking it for granted I felt the same as he did. This is a very engaging quality of his, and makes one feel sympathetic, especially when he looks into one's eyes with his sleepy blue ones. He has lashes as long and curly as a gipsy's baby.

Mr. Carruthers was alone in the dining-room when I got in; he was looking out of the window, and turned round sharply as I came up the room. I am sure he would like to have been killing flies on the panes if he had been a boy! His eyes were steel.

" Where have you been all the time ?" he asked, when he had shaken hands and said good- morning.

" Up in my room packing," I said simply. " Lord Robert was so kind, he helped me|we|have got everything done, and may I order the carriage for the 5.15 train, please ?"

" Certainly not|confound Lord Robert! " Mr. Carruthers said. " What business is it of his? You are not to go. I won't let you. Dear, silly, little child|" his voice was quite moved. " You can't possibly go out into the world all alone. EVangeline, why won't you marry me ? I|do you know, I believe|I shall love you "

" I should have to be *perfectly sure* that the person I married loved me, Mr. Carruthers," I said, demurely, " before I consented to finish up my life like that."

He had no time to answer, for Mr. Barton and Lord Robert came into the room.

There seemed a gloom over luncheon. There were pauses, and Lord Robert had a more pathetic expression than ever. His hands are a nice shape|but so are Mr. Carruthers', they both look very much like gentlemen.

Before we had finished, a note was brought in to me. It was from Lady Katherine Mont- gomerie. She was too sorry, she said, to hear of my lonely position, and she was writing to ask if I would not come over and spend a fortnight with them at Tryland Court.

It was not well worded, and I had never cared much for Lady Katherine, but it was fairly kind, and fitted in perfectly with my plans.

She had probably heard of Mr. Carruthers' arrival, and was scandalized at my being alone in the house with him.

Both men had their eyes fixed on my face when I looked up, as I finished reading the note.

"Lady Katherine Montgomerie writes to ask me to Tryland," I said; " so if you will excuse me I will answer it, and say I will come this afternoon,"|and I got up.

Mr. Carruthers rose too, and followed me into the library. He deliberately shut the door and came over to the writing-table where I sat down.

" Well, if I let you go, will you tell her then that you are engaged to me, and I am going to marry you as soon as possible."

" No, indeed I won't! " I said, decidedly.

" I am not going to marry you, or any one, Mr. Carruthers. What do you think of me|! Fancy my consenting to come back here for ever, and live with you|when I don't know you a bit|and having to put up with your| perhaps|kissing me, and, and|things of that sort! It is perfectly dreadful to think of!"

He laughed as if in spite of himself. " But supposing I promised not to kiss you ?"

" EVen so," I said, and I couldn't help biting the end of my pen, " it could happen that I might get a feeling I wanted to kiss some one else|and there it is! Once you're married, everything nice is wrong! "

" EVangeline ! I won't let you go|out of my life|you strange little witch, you have upset me, disturbed me, I can settle to nothing. I seem to want you so very much."

" Pouff! " I said, and I pouted at him.

" You have everything in your life to fill it |position, riches, friends|you don't want a green-eyed adventuress."

I bent down and wrote steadily to Lady Katherine. I would be there about 6 o'clock, I said, and thanked her in my best style.

" If I let you go, it is only for the time," Mr. Carruthers said, as I signed my name. " I *intend* you to marry me|do you hear! "

" Again I say *qui vivra verra!* " I laughed, and rose with the note in my hand.

Lord Robert looked almost ready to cry when I told him I was off in the afternoon.

"I shall see you again," he said. "Lady Katherine is a relation of my aunt's husband, Lord Merrenden. I don't know her myself, though."

I do not believe him|how can he see me again|young men do talk a lot of nonsense.

" I shall come over on Wednesday to see how you are getting on," Mr. Carruthers said. " Please do be in."

I promised I would, and then I came upstairs.

And so it has come to an end, my life at Branches. I am going to start a new phase of existence, my first beginning as an adventuress!

How completely all one's ideas can change in a few days. This day three weeks ago Mrs. Carruthers was alive. This day two weeks ago I found myself no longer a prospective heiress| and only three days ago I was contemplating calmly the possibility of marrying Mr. Carruthers|and now|for heaven|I would not marry any one! And so, for fresh woods and pastures new. Oh! I want to see the world, and lots of different human beings|I want to know what it is makes the clock go round| that great, big, clock of life|I want to dance, and to sing, and to laugh, and to *live*|and| and|yes|perhaps some day to kiss some one I love !

3

SECTION 3

Tryland Court, Headington,
  Wednesday, November)th.
  Goodness gracious! I have been here four whole days, and I continually ask myself how I shall be able to stand it for the rest of the fortnight. Before I left Branches I began to have a sinking at the heart. There were horribly touching farewells with housekeepers and people I have known since a child, and one hates to have that choky feeling|especially as just at the end of it|while tears were still in my eyes, Mr. Carruthers came out into the hall, and saw them|so did Lord Robert!

I blinked, and blinked, but one would trickle down my nose. It was a horribly awkward moment.

Mr. Carruthers made profuse inquiries as to my comforts for the drive, in a tone colder than ever, and insisted upon my drinking some cherry brandy. Such fussing is quite unlike his usual manner, so I suppose he too felt it was a tiresome *quart d'heure.* Lord Robert didnot hide his concern, he came up to me and took my hand while Christopher was speaking to the footman who was going with me.

" You are a dear," he said, " and a brick, and don't you forget I shall come and stay with Lady Katherine before you leave, so you won't feel you are all among strangers."

I thanked him, and he squeezed my hand so kindly|I do like Lord Robert.

Very soon I was gay again, and *insouciante,* and the last they saw of me was smiling out of the brougham window as I drove *off* in the dusk. They both stood upon the steps and waved to me.

Tea was over at Tryland when I arrived, such a long, damp drive! And I explained to Lady Katherine how sorry I was to have had to come so late, and that I could not think of troubling her to have up fresh for me|but she insisted, and after a while a whole new lot came, made in a hurry with the water not boiling, and I had to gulp down a nasty cup| Ceylon tea, too|I hate Ceylon tea! Mr. Mont- gomerie warmed himself before the fire, quite shielding it from us, who shivered on a row of high-backed chairs beyond the radius of the hearth rug.

He has a way of puffing out his cheeks and making a noise like " Bur-r-r-r "|which sounds very bluff and hearty, until you find he has said a mean thing about some one directly after. And while red hair looks very well on me, I do think a man with it is the ugliest thing in creation. His face is red, and his nose and cheeks almost purple, and fiery whiskers, fierce enough to frighten a cat *in a.* dark lane.

He was a rich Scotch manufacturer, and poor Lady Katherine had to marry him, I suppose, though, as she is Scotch herself, I daresay she does not notice that he is rather coarse.

There are two sons and six daughters, one married, four grown-up, and one at school in Brussels, and all with red hair!|but straight and coarse, and with freckles and white eyelashes. So really it is very kind of Lady Katherine to have asked me here.

They are all as good as gold on top, and one does poker work, and another binds books and a third embroiders altar-cloths, and the fourth knits ties|all for charities, and they ask everyone to subscribe to them directly they come to the house. The tie and the altar-cloth one were sitting working hard in the drawing- room|Kirstie and Jean are their names| Jessie and Maggie, the poker worker and the bookbinder have a sitting-room to themselves, their workshop they call it. They were there still, I suppose, for I did not see them until dinner. We used to meet once a year at Mrs. Carruthers' Christmas parties ever since ages and ages, and I remember I hated their tartan sashes, and they generally had colds in their heads, and one year they gave every one mumps, so they were not asked the next. The altar- cloth one, Jean, is my age, the other three are older.

It was really very difficult to find something to say, and I can quite understand common people fidgeting when they feel worried like this. I have never fidgeted since eight years ago, the last time Mrs. Carruthers boxed my ears for it. Just before going up to dress for dinner Mr. Montgomerie asked blank out if it was true that Mr. Carruthers had arrived. Lady Katherine had been skirting round this subject for a quarter of an hour.

I only said yes, but that was not enough, and once started, he asked a string of questions, with " Bur-r-r-r " several times in between. Was Mr. Carruthers going to shoot the pheasants in November? Had he decided to keep on the *chef?* Had he given up diplomacy ? I said I really did not know any of these things, I had seen so little of him.

Lady Katherine nodded her head, while she measured a comforter she was knitting to see if it was long enough.

"I am sure it must have been most awkward for you, his arriving at all; it was not very good taste on his part, I am afraid, but I suppose he wished to see his inheritance as soon as possible," she said.

I nearly laughed, thinking what she would say if she knew which part of his inheritance he had really come to see. I do wonder if she has ever heard that Mrs. Carruthers left me to him, more or less, in her will!

" I hope you had your old governess with you, at least," she continued, as we went up the stairs, " so that you could feel less uncomfortable|really a most shocking situation for a girl alone in the house with an unmarried man."

I told her Mr. Barton was there too, but I had not the courage to say anything about Lord Robert; only that Mr. Carruthers had a friend of his down, who was a great judge of pictures, to see them.

" Oh ! a valuer, I suppose. I hope he is not going to sell the Correggios!" she exclaimed.

" No, I don't think so," I said, leaving the part about the valuer unanswered.

Mr. Carruthers, being unmarried, seemed to worry her most; she went on about it again before we got to my bedroom door.

" I happened to hear a rumour at Miss

Sheriton's (the wool shop in Headington, our

town), this morning," she said, " and so I

wrote at once to you. I felt how terrible it would be for one of my own dear girls to be left alone with a bachelor like that|I almost wonder you did not stay up in your own rooms."

I thanked her for her kind thought, and she left me at last!

If she only knew! The unmarried ones who came down the passage to talk to Mademoiselle were not half so saucy as the old fellows with wives somewhere. Lord Bentworth was married, and he wanted me to kiss him, whereas Colonel Grimston had no wife, and he never said bo! to a goose! And I do wonder what she thought Mr. Carruthers was going to do to me, that it would have been wiser for me to stay up in my rooms. Perhaps she thinks diplomats, having lived in foreign places, are sort of wild beasts.

My room is frightful after my pretty rosy chintzes at Branches. Nasty yellowish wood furniture, and nothing much matching; however there are plenty of wardrobes, so Veron- ique is content.

They were all in the drawing-room when I got down, and Malcolm, the eldest son, who is in a Highland Militia regiment, had arrived by a seven o'clock train.

I had that dreadful feeling of being very late, and Mr. Montgomerie wanting to swear at me, though it was only a minute past a quarter to eight.

He said " Bur-r-r " several times, and flew off to the dining-room with me tucked under his arm, murmuring it gave no cook a chance to keep the dinner waiting! So I expected something wonderful in the way of food, but it is not half so good as our *chef* gave us at Branches. And the footmen are not all the same height, and their liveries don't fit like Mrs. Carruthers always insisted that ours should do.

Malcolm *is* a tittsy-pootsy man ! Not as tall as I am, and thin as a rail, with a look of his knees being too near together. He must be awful in a kilt, and I am sure he shivers when the wind blows, he has that air. I don't like kilts, unless men are big, strong, bronzed creatures who don't seem ashamed of their bare bits. I saw some splendid specimens marching once in Edinburgh, and they swung their skirts just like the beautiful ladies in the Bois, when Mademoiselle and I went out of the Alice Mrs. Carruthers told us to try always to walk in.

Lady Katherine talked a great deal at dinner about politics, and her different charities, and the four girls were so respectful and interested, but Mr. Montgomerie contradicted her whenever he could. I was glad when we went into the drawing-room.

That first evening was the worst of all, because we were all so strange; one seems to get acclimatized to whatever it is after a while.

Lady Katherine asked me if I had not some fancy work to do. Kirstie had begun her ties, and Jean the altar-cloth again.

"Do let Maggie run to your room and fetch it for you," she said.

I was obliged to tell her I never did any. " But I|I can trim hats," I said. It really seemed so awful not to be able to do anything like them, I felt I must say this as a kind of defence for myself.

However, she seemed to think that hardly a lady's employment.

" How clever of you! " Kirstie exclaimed. " I wish I could; but don't you find that intermittent ? You can't trim them all the time. Don't you feel the want of a constant employment?"

I was obliged to say I had not felt like that yet, but I could not tell them I particularly loved sitting perfectly still, doing nothing.

Jessie and Maggie played Patience at two tables which folded up, and which they brought out, and sat down to with a deliberate accustomed look, which made me know at once they did this every night, and that I should see those tables planted exactly on those two spots of carpet each evening during my whole stay. I suppose it is because they cannot bring the poker work and the bookbinding into the drawing-room.

"Won't you play us something?" Lady Katherine asked, plaintively. EVidently it was not permitted to do nothing, so I got up and went to the piano.

Fortunately I know heaps of things by heart, and I love them, and would have gone on, and on, so as to fill up the time, but they all said " thank you " in a chorus after each bit, and it rather put me off.

Mr. Montgomerie and Malcolm did not come in for ages, and I could see Lady Katherine getting uneasy. One or two things at dinner suggested to me that these two were not on the best terms, perhaps she feared they had come to blows in the dining-room. The Scotch, Mrs. Carruthers said, have all kinds of rough customs that other nations do not keep up any longer.

They did turn up at last, and Mr. Montgomerie was purple all over his face, and Malcolm a pale green, but there were no bruises on him ; only one could see they had had a terrible quarrel.

There is something in breeding after all, even if one is of a barbarous country. Lady Katherine behaved so well, and talked charities

4

SECTION 4

and politics faster than ever, and did not give them time for any further outburst, though I fancy I heard a few " dams " mixed with the " bur-r-r-rs," and not without the " n " on just for ornament, like Lord Robert's. It was a frightful evening.

Wednesday, Nov.)th (continued).

Malcolm walked beside me going to church the next day. He looked a little less depressed and I tried to cheer him up.

He did not tell me what his worries were, but Jean had said something about it when she came into my room as I was getting ready. It appears he has got into trouble over a horse called Angela Grey. Jean gathered this from Lady Katherine, she said her father was very angry about it, as he had spent so much money on it.

To me it does not sound like a horse's name,

and I told Jean so, but she was perfectly

horrified, and said it must be a horse, because

they were not acquainted with any AngelaGrey, and did not even know any Greys at all: so it must be a horse!

I think that a ridiculous reason, as Mrs. Carruthers said all young men knew people one wouldn't want toland it was silly to make a fuss about itland that they couldn't help itland they would be very dull if they were as good as gold like girls.

But I expect Lady Katherine thinks differently about things to Mrs. Carruthers, and the daughters are the same.

I shall ask Lord Robert when I see him again if it is a horse or no.

Malcolm is not attractive, and I was glad the church was not far off.

No carriages are allowed out on Sunday, so we had to walk, and coming back it began to rain, and we could not go round the stables, which I understand is the custom here every Sunday.

Everything is done because it is the custom lnot because you want to amuse yourself.

" When it rains and we can't go round the stables," Kirstie said, "we look at the old ' Illustrated London News,' and go there on our way from afternoon church."

I did not particularly want to do that, so stayed in my room as long as I could. The four girls were seated at a large table in the hall, each with a volume in front of her when I got down at last. They must know every picture by heart, if they do it every Sunday it rainslthey stay in England all the winter!

Jean made room for me beside her.

" I am at the ' Sixties,' " she said. " I finished the 'Fifties' last Easter." So they evidently do even this with a method.

I asked her if there were not any new books they wanted to read, but she said Lady Katherine did not care for their looking at magazines or novels unless she had been through them first, and she had not time for many, so they kept the few they had to read between tea and dinner on Sunday.

By this time I felt I should do something wicked; and if the luncheon gong had not sounded, I do not know what would have happened.

Mr. Montgomerie said rather gallant things to me when the cheese and port came along, while the girls looked shocked, and Lady Katherine had a stony stare. I suppose he is like this because he is married. I wonder, though, if young married men are the same, I have never met any yet.

By Monday night I was beginning to feel the end of the world would come soon ! It is ten times worse than even having had to conceal all my feelings, and abjectly obey Mrs. Carruthers. Because she did say cynical, entertaining things sometimes to me, and to her friends, that made one laugh. And one felt it was only she who made the people who were dependent upon her do her way, because she, herself, was so selfish, and that the rest of the world were free if once one got outside.

But Lady Katherine, and the whole Montgomerie *milieu,* give you the impression that everything and everybody must be ruled by rules; and no one could have a right to an individual opinion in any sphere of society.

You simply can't laugh, they asphyxiate you. I am looking forward to this afternoon, and Mr. Carruthers coming over. I often think of the days at Branches, and how exciting it was, with those two, and I wish I were back again.

I have tried to be polite and nice to them all here, and yet they don't seem absolutely pleased.

Malcolm gazes at me with sheep's eyes. They are a washy blue, with the family white eyelashes (how different to Lord Robert's!). He has the most precise, regulated manner, and never says a word of slang, he ought to have been a young curate, and I can't imagine him spending his money on any Angela Greys, even if she is a horse or not.

He speaks to me when he can, and asks me to go for walks round the golf course. The four girls play for an hour and three-quarters every morning. They never seem to enjoy anything|the whole of life is a solid duty. I am sitting up in my room, and Veronique has had the sense to have my fire lighted early. I suppose Mr. Carruthers won't come until about four, an hour more to begot through. I have said I must write letters, and so have escaped from them, and not had to go for the usual drive.

I suppose he will have the sense to ask for me, even if Lady Katherine is not back when he comes.

This morning it was so fine and frosty a kind of devil seemed to creep into me. I have been *so* good since Saturday, so when Malcolm said, in his usual prim, priggish voice, " Miss Travers, may I have the pleasure of taking you for a little exercise," I jumped up without consulting Lady Katherine, and went and put my things on, and we started.

I had a feeling that they were all thinking I was doing something wrong, and so, of course, it made me worse. I said every kind of simple thing I could to Malcolm to make him jump, and looked at him now and then from under my eyelashes. So when we got to a stile, he did want to help me! and his eyes were quite wobblish! He has a giggle right up in the treble, and it comes out at such unexpected moments, when there is nothing to laugh at. I suppose it is being Scotch, he has just caughtthemeaning of some former joke. Therewould never be any use in saying things to him like to Lord Robert and Mr. Carruthers, because one would have left the place before he understood, if even then.

There was an old Sir Thomas Farquharson who came to Branches, and he grasped the deepest jokes of Mrs. Carruthers, so deep that even I did not understand them, and he was Scotch. It may be they are like that only when they have red hair.

When I was seated on top of a stile, Malcolm suddenly announced, " I hear you are going to London when you go. I hope you will let me come and see you, but I wish you lived here always."

" I don't," I said, and then I remembered that sounded rather rude, and they had been kind to me. "At least|you know, I think the country is dull|don't you|for always ?"

" Yes," he replied, primly, " for men, but it is where I should always wish to see the woman I respected."

" Are towns so wicked ?" I asked, in my little angel voice. " Tell me of their pitfalls, so that I may avoid them."

" You must not believe everything people say to you, to begin with," he said, seriously. " For one so young as you, I am afraid you will find your path beset with temptations."

" Oh ! do tell me what! " I implored. " I have always wanted to know what temptations were. Please tell me. If you come to see me |would you be a temptation, or is temptation a thing, and not a person ? " I looked at him so beseechingly, he never for a second saw the twinkle in my eye!

He coughed pompously. " I expect I should be," he said, modestly. " Temptations arel erlerlOh ! I say, you know, I saylI don't know what to say "

" Oh, what a pity! " I said, regretfully. " I was hoping to hear all about it from youl specially if you are one yourself, you must know "

He looked gratified, but still confused.

" You see when you are quite alone in London, some man may make love to you."

" Oh! do you think so *really* ?" I asked, aghast. " That, I suppose would be frightful, if I were by myself in the room ! Would it be all right, do you think, if I left the sitting-room door open, and kept Veronique on the other side?"

He looked at me hard, but he only saw the face of an unprotected angel, and, becoming reassured, he said gravely,

" Yes, it might be just as well! "

" You do surprise me about love," I said. " I had no idea it was a violent kind of thing like that. I thought it began with grave reverence and respectland after years of offering flowers and humble compliments, and bread and butter at tea-parties, the gentleman went down upon one knee and made a declarationl ' Clara, Maria, I adore you, be mine,' and then one put out a lily-white hand, and, blushing, told him to riselbut that can't be your sort, and you have not yet explained what temptation means ?"

" It means more or less wanting to do what you ought not to."

"Oh, then ! " I said, " I am having temptation all the time, aren't you? For instance, I want to tear up Jean's altar-cloths, and rip Kirstie's ties, and tool bad words on Jessie's bindings, and burn Maggie's wood boxes! "

He looked horribly shockedland hurtl so I added at oncel

" Of course it must be lovely to be able to do these things, they are perfect girls, and so cleverlonly it makes me feel like that because I suppose I amldifferent."

He looked at me critically. " Yes, you are different, I wish you would try to be more like my sisterslthen I should not feel so nervous about your going to London.

"It is too good of you to worry," I said, demurely; "but I don't think you need, you know! I have rather a strong suspicion I am acquainted with the way to take care of myself! " and I bent down and laughed right in his face, and jumped off the stile on to the other side.

He did look such a teeny shrimp climbing after me! but it does not matter what is theirsize, the vanity of men is just the same. I am sure he thought he had only to begin making love to me himself, and I would drop like a ripe peach into his mouth.

I teased him all the way back, until when we got into lunch he did not know whether he was on his head or his heels! Just as we came up to the door, he said:

" I thought your name was EVangelinel why did you say it was Clara Maria ?"

" Becauselit is not!! " I laughed over my shoulder, and ran into the house.

He stood on the steps, and if he had been one of the stable boys he would have scratched his head.

Now I must stop and dress. I shall put on a black tea frock I have. Mr. Carruthers shall see I have not caught frumpdom from my hosts!

Night.

I do think men are the most horrid creatures,

you can't believe what they say, or rely upon
them for five minutes! Mrs. Carruthers was
right, she said, " Evangeline, remember, it isquite difficult enough to trust oneself, without trusting a man."

Such an afternoon I have had! That annoying feeling of waiting for something all the time, and nothing happening. For Mr. Car- ruthers did not turn up after all! How I wish I had not dressed and expected him.

He is probably saying to himself he is well out of the business|now I have gone. I don't suppose he meant a word of his protestations to me. Well, he need not worry! I had no intention of jumping down his throat|only I would have been glad to see him because he is human, and not like any one here.

Of course Lord Robert will be the same, and I shall probably never see either of them again. How can Lord Robert get here, when he does not know Lady Katherine. No, it was just said to say something nice when I was leaving, and he will be as horrid as Mr. Carruthers.

I am thankful at least that I did not tell Lady Katherine, I should have felt such a goose. Oh! I do wonder what I shall do next. I don't know at all how much things cost|perhaps three hundred a year is very poor. I am sure my best frocks always were five or six hundred francs each, and I daresay hotels run away with money. But, for the moment, I am rich, as Mr. Barton kindly advanced some of my legacy to me, and oh! I am going to see life! and it is absurd to be sad ! I shall go to bed, and forget how cross I feel!

They are going to have a shoot here next week|Pheasants. I wonder if they will have a lot of old men. I have not heard all who are coming.

Lady Katherine said to me after dinner this evening that she was sorry as she was afraid it would be most awkward for me their having a party, on account of my deep mourning, and I, if I felt it dreadfully, I need not consider they would find me the least rude if I preferred to have dinner in my room!

I don't want to have dinner in my room! Think of the stuffiness of it! and perhaps hearing laughter going on downstairs.

I can always amuse myself watching faces, however dull tney are. I thanked her, and said it would not be at all necessary, as I must get accustomed to seeing people, I could not count upon always meeting hostesses with such kind thoughts as hers, and I might as well get used to it.

She said yes, but not cordially.

To-morrow Mrs. Mackintosh, the eldest daughter, is arriving with her four children. I remember her wedding five years ago. I have never seen her since.

She was very tall and thin, and stooped dreadfully, and Mrs. Carruthers said Providence had been very kind in giving her a husband at all. But when Mr. Mackintosh trotted down the aisle with her, I did not think so!

A wee sandy fellow about up to her shoulder !

Oh, I would hate to be tied to that! I think to be tied to anything could not be very nice. I wonder how I ever thought of marrying Mr. Carruthers off hand!

I feel now I shall never marry|for years. Of course, one can't be an old maid! But for a long time I mean to see life first.

5

SECTION 5

Tryland,
> *Thursday, Nov. loth.*
> " Branches, *Wednesday.*

" Dear Miss Travers,ǀI regret exceedingly I was unable to come over to Tryland to-day, but hope to do so before you leave. I trust you are well, and did not catch cold on the drive.

"Yours very truly, "christopher Carruthers."

'This is what I get this morning! Pig!

Well, I sha'n't be in if he does comeǀI can just see him pulling himself together once temptation (it makes me think of Malcolm !), is out of his way; he no doubt feels he has had an escape, as I am nobody very grand.

The letters come early here, as everywhere, but in a bag which only Mr. Montgomerie can open, and one has to wait until everyone is seated at breakfast before he produces the key, and deals them all out.

Mr. Carruthers' was the only one for me, and it had "Branches" on the envelope, which attracted Mr. Montgomerie's attention, and he began to " Bur-r-r-r," and hardly gave me time to read it before he commenced to ask questions J *prof os* of the place, to get me to say what the letter was about. He is a curious man.

" Carruthers is a capital fellow, they tell me |er|You had better ask him over quietly, Katherine, if he is all alone at Branches" |this with one eye on me in a questioning way.

I remained silent.

" Perhaps he is off to London, though ?"

I pretended to be busy with my coffee.

" Best pheasant shoot in the county, and a close borough under the old *regime'*, hope he will be more neighbourly|er|suppose he must shoot 'em before December ?"

I buttered my toast.

Then the " Bur-r-r-rs " began !! I wonder he does not have a noise that ends with d|n simply, it would save him time!

" Couldn't help seeing your letter was fromBranches. Hope Carruthers gives you some news ?"

As he addressed me deliberately I was obliged to answer:

" I have no information. It is only a business letter," and I ate toast again.

He " bur-r-r-d" more than ever, and opened some of his own correspondence.

" What am I to do, Katherine ?" he said, presently; " that confounded fellow Campion has thrown me over for next week, and he is my best gun: at short notice like this, it's impossible to replace him with the same class of shot."

" Yes, dear," said Lady Katherine, in that kind of voice that has not heard the question |she was deep in her own letters.

" Katherine ! " roared Mr. Montgomerie. " Will you listen when I speak|Bur-r-r! " and he thumped his fist on the table.

Poor Lady Katherine almost jumped, and the china raided.

" Forgive me, Anderson," she said, humbly, " you were saying ?"

" Campion has thrown me over," glared Mr. Montgomerie.

" Then I have perhaps the very thing for you," Lady Katherine said, in a relieved way, returning to her letters. " Sophia Merrenden writes this morning, and among other things tells me of her nephew, Lord Robert Vavasour |you know, Torquilstone's half-brother. She says he is the most charming young man, and a wonderful shot|she even suggests " (looking back a page), " that he might be useful to us, if we are short of a gun."

"Damned kind of her," growled Mr. Montgomerie.

I hope they did not notice, but I had suddenly such a thrill of pleasure that I am sure my cheeks got red. I felt frightfully excited to hear what was going to happen.

" Merrenden, as you know, is the best judge of shooting in England," Lady Katherine went on, in an injured voice. " Sophia is hardly likely to recommend his nephew so highly if he were not pretty good."

"But you don't know the puppy, Katherine."My heart fell.

" That is not the least consequence|we are almost related. Merrenden is my first cousin, you forget that, I suppose! "

Fortunately I could detect that Lady Kath- erine was becoming obstinate and offended. I drank some more coffee. Oh! how lovely if Lord Robert comes!

Mr. Montgomerie "Bur-r-r-ed " a lot first, but Lady Katherine got him round, and before breakfast was over, it was decided she should write to Lord Robert, and ask him to come to the shoot. As we were all standing looking out of the window at the dripping rain, I heard her say in a low voice,

" Really, Anderson, we must think of the girls sometimes. Torquilstone is a confirmed bachelor and a cripple|Lord Robert will certainly one day be Duke."

" Well, catch him if you can," said Mr. Montgomerie. He is coarse sometimes !

I am not going to let myself think much about Lord Robert|Mr. Carruthers has been a lesson to me|but if he does come|I wonder|if Lady Katherine will think it funny of me not saying I knew him when she first spoke of him. It is too late now, so it can't be helped.

The Mackintosh party arrived this afternoon. Marriage must have quite different effects on some people. Numbers of the married women we saw in London were lovely, prettier, I always heard, than they had been before|but Mary Mackintosh is perfectly awful. She can't be more than twenty-seven, but she looks forty, at least; and stout, and sticking out all in the wrong places, and flat where the stick-outs ought to be. And the four children! The two eldest look much the same age, the next a little smaller, and there is a baby, and they all squall, and although they seem to have heaps of nurses, poor Mr. Mackintosh has to be a kind of under one. He fetches and carries for them, and gives his handkerchief when they slobber|but perhaps it is he feels proud that a person of his size had these four enormous babies almost all at once like that.

The whole thing is simply dreadful.

Tea was a pandemonium! The four aunts gushing over the infants, and feeding them with cake,and gurgling with "Tootsie-wootsie- popsy-wopsy " kind of noises. They will get to do " Bur-r-r-rs" I am sure, when they grow older. I wonder if the infants will come down every afternoon when the shoot happens. The guests will enjoy it!

I said to Jean as we came upstairs that I thought it seemed terrible to get married| did not she ? But she was shocked, and said no, marriage and motherhood were sacred duties, and she envied her sister!

This kind of thing is not my idea of bliss. Two really well-behaved children would be delicious, I think; but four squalling imps all about the same age is *bourgeois,* and not the affair of a lady.

I suppose Lord Robert's answer cannot get here till about Saturday. I wonder how he arranged it! It is clever of him. Lady Katherine said this Mr. Campion who was coming is in the same regiment, the 3rd Life Guards. Perhaps when|but there is no use my thinking about it|only somehow I am feeling so much better to-night|gay, and as if I did not mind being very poor|that I was obliged to tease Malcolm a little after dinner. I *would* play Patience, and never lifted my eyes from the cards! He kept trying to say things to me to get me to go to the piano, but I pretended I did not notice. A palm stands at the corner of a high Chippendale writing bureau, and Jessie happened to have put the Patience table behind that rather, so the rest of them could not see everything that was happening. Malcolm at last sat very near beside me, and wanted to help with the aces|but I can't bear people being close to me, so I upset the board, and he had to pick up all the cards on the floor. Kirstie, for a wonder, played the piano then| a cake walk|and there was something in it that made me feel I wanted to move|to dance|to undulate|I don't know what, and my shoulders swayed a little in time to the music. Malcolm breathed quite as if he had a cold, and said right in my ear, in a fat voice, " You know you are a devil|and I "

I stopped him at once|looked up for the first time, absolutely shocked and surprised.

" Really, Mr. Montgomerie, I do not know what you mean," I said.

He began to fidget.

" Er|I mean|I mean|I awfully wish to kiss you."

" But I do not a bit wish to kiss you ! " I said, and I opened my eyes wide at him.

He looked like a spiteful bantam, and fortunately at that moment Jessie returned to the Patience, and he could not say any more.

Lady Katherine and Mrs. Mackintosh came into my room on the way up to bed. She| Lady Katherine|wanted to show Mary how beautifully they had had it done up, it used to be hers before she married. They looked all round at the dead-daffbdil-coloured cretonne and things, and at last I could see their eyes often straying to my night-gown and dressing- gown, laid out on a chair beside the fire.

" Oh, Lady Katherine, I am afraid you are|wondering at my having pink silk," I said, apologetically, " as I am in mourning, but I have not had time to get a white dressing-gown yet."

" It is not that, dear," said Lady Katherine, in a grave duty voice. " I|I|do not think such a night-gown is suitable for a girl."

" Oh! but I am very strong," I said. " I never catch cold."

Mary Mackintosh held it up, with a face of stern disapproval. Of course it has short sleeves ruffled with Valenciennes, and is fine linen cambric nicely embroidered. Mrs. Car- ruthers was always very particular about them, and chose them herself at Doucet's. She said one never could know when places might catch on fire.

" Evangeline, dear, you are very young, so you probably cannot understand," Mary said, " but I consider this garment not in any way fit for a girl|or for any good woman for that matter. Mother, I hope my sisters have not seen it!!"

I looked so puzzled.

She examined the stuff, one could see the chair through it, beyond.

" What *would* Alexander say if I were to wear such a thing! "

This thought seemed almost to suffocate them both, they looked genuinely pained and shocked.

" Of course it would be too tight for you," I said, humbly, " but it is otherwise a very good pattern, and does not tear when one puts up one's arms. Mrs. Carruthers made a fuss at Doucet's because my last set tore so soon, and they altered these."

At the mention of my late adopted mother, both of them pulled themselves up.

" Mrs. Carruthers we know had very odd notions," Lady Katherine said stiffly, " but I hope, Evangeline, you have sufficient sense to understand now for yourself that such a|a| garment is not at all seemly."

" Oh! why not, dear Lady Katherine ?" I said. " You don't know how becoming it is."

"Becoming!" almost screamed Mary Mack

6

SECTION 6

intosh. " But no nice-minded woman wants things to look becoming in bed! "

The whole matter appeared so painful to them I covered up the offending ' nighty' with my dressing-gown, and coughed. It made a break, and they went away, saying good-night frigidly.

And now I am alone. But I do wonder why it is wrong to look pretty in bed,|considering nobody sees one, too!

Tryland Court,

Monday, November ith.

I Have not felt like writing; these last days have been so stodgy,|sticky I was going to say! Endless infant talk ! The methods of head nurses, teething, the knavish tricks of nursemaids, patent foods, bottles, bibs|everything! Enough to put one off for ever from wishing to get married ! And Mary Mackintosh sitting there all out of shape, expounding theories that can have no results in practice, as there could not be worse behaved children than hers!

They even try Lady Katherine, I can see, when the two eldest, who come in while we are at breakfast each day, take the jam spoon, or something equally horrid, and dab it all over the cloth. Yesterday they put their hands in the honey dish which Mr. Montgomerie was helping himself to, and then after smearing him (the "Bur-r-r-s" were awful) they went round the table to escape being caught, and fingered the back of every one's chair, and the door handle, so that one could not touch a thing without getting sticky.

" Alexander, dearie," Mary said, " Alec must have his mouth wiped."

Poor Mr. Mackintosh had to get up and leave his breakfast, catch these imps, and employ his table-napkin in vain.

" Take 'em upstairs, do, Bur-r-r-r," roared their fond grandfather.

" Oh, father, the poor darlings are not really naughty!" Mary said, offended. " I like them to be with us all as much as possible. I thought they would be such a pleasure to you."

Upon which, hearing the altercation, both infants set up a yell of fear and rage, and Alec, the cherub of four and a half, lay on the floor and kicked and screamed until he was black in the face.

Mr. Mackintosh is too small to manage two, so one of the footmen had to come and help him to carry them up to their nursery! Oh, I would not be in his place for the world!

Malcolm is becoming so funny! I suppose he is attracted by me. He makes kind of love in a priggish way whenever he gets the chance, which is not often, as Lady Katherine contrives to send one of the girls with us on all our walks, or if we are in the drawing-room she comes and sits down beside us herself. I am glad, as it would be a great bore to listen to a quantity of it.

How silly of her, though ! She can't know as much about men as even I do!of course it only makes him all the more eager.

It is quite an object lesson for me. I shall be impossibly difficult myself if I meet Mr. Carruthers again, as he has no mother to play these tricks for him.

7

SECTION 7

Lord Robert's answer came on Saturday afternoon. It was all done through Lady Merrenden.

He will be delighted to come and shoot on Tuesday|to-morrow. Oh ! I am so glad| but I do wonder if I shall be able to make him understand not to say anything about having been at Branches while I was there. Such a simple thing, but Lady Katherine is so odd and particular.

The party is to be a large one, nine guns| I hope some will be amusing, though I rather fear!

Tuesday night

It is quite late, nearly twelve o'clock, but I feel so wide awake I must write.

I shall begin from the beginning, when every one arrived.

They came by two trains early in the afternoon, and just at tea time, and Lord Robert was among the last lot.

They are mostly the same sort as Lady Katherine, looking as good as gold; but one woman. Lady Verningham, Lady Katherine's niece, is different, and I liked her at once.

She has lovely clothes, and an exquisite figure, and her hat on the right way. She has charming manners too, but one can see she is on a duty visit.

Even all this company did not altogether stop Mary Mackintosh laying down the law upon domesticlinfant domesticlaffairs. We all sat in the big drawing-room, and I caught Lady Verningham's eye, and we laughed together! The first eye with a meaning in it I have seen since I left Branches.

Everybody talked so agreeably, with pauses, not enjoying themselves at all, when Jean and Kirstie began about their work, and explained it, and tried to get orders, and Jessie and Maggie too, and specimens of it all had to be shown, and prices fixed. I should hate to have to beg, even for a charity.

I felt quite uncomfortable for them, but they did not mind a bit, and their victims were noble over it.

Our parson at Branches always got so red and nervous when he had to ask for anything; one could see he was quite a gentlemanlbut women are different, I suppose.

I longed for tea!

While they are all very kind here, there is that asphyxiating atmosphere of stiffness and decorum which affects every one who comes to Tryland. A sort of " The gold must be tried by fire, and the heart must be wrung by pain " kind of suggestion about everything.

They are extraordinarily cheerful, because it is a Christian virtue, cheerfulness; not because they are brimming over with joy, or that lovely feeling of being alive, and not minding much what happens, you feel so splendid, like I get on fine days.

Everything they do has a reason or a moral in it. This party is because pheasants have to be killed in Novemberland certain people have to be entertained, and their charities can be assisted through them. Oh ! if I had a big house, and were rich, I would have lovely parties, with all sorts of nice people, because I wanted to give them a good time and laugh myself. Lady Verningham was talking to me just before tea, when the second train load arrived.

I tried to be quite indifferent, but I did feel dreadfully excited when Lord Robert walked in. Oh! he looked such a beautiful creature, so smart, and straight, and lithe!

Lady Katherine was frightfully stiff with him ; it would have discouraged most people, but that is the lovely part about Lord Robert, he is always absolutely *sans glne*

He saw me at once, of course, and came over as straight as a die the moment he could.

" How do, Robert! " said Lady Verningham, looking very surprised to see him, and giving him her fingers in such an attractive way. *How* are you here ? And why is our Campie not? Thereby hangs some tale, I feel sure! "

" Why, yes !" said Lord Robert, and he held her hand. Then he looked at me with his eyebrows up. "But won't you introduce me to Miss Travers? to my great chagrin she seems to have forgotten me! "

I laughed,and Lady Verningham introduced us, and he sat down beside us, and every one began tea.

Lady Verningham had such a look in her eye!

" Robert, tell me about it! " she said.

" I hear they have five thousand pheasants to slay," Lord Robert replied, looking at her with his innocent smile.

" Robert, you are lying! " she said, and she laughed. She is so pretty when she laughs, not very young, over thirty I should think, but such a charm ! As different as different can be from the whole Montgomerie family!

I hardly spoke, they continued to tease one another, and Lord Robert ate most of a plate of bread and butter that was near.

" I am dam'd hungry, Lady Ver! " he said. She smiled at him; she evidently likes him very much.

" Robert! you must not use such language here! " she said.

" Oh, doesn't he say them often! those dams! " I burst out, not thinking for a momentIthen I stopped, remembering. She did seem surprised.

" So you have heard them before! I thought you had only just met casually!" she said, with such a comic look of understanding, but not absolutely pleased. I stupidly got crimson, it did annoy me, because it shows so dreadfully on my skin. She leant back in her chair, and laughed.

" It is delightful to shoot five thousand pheasants, Robert," she said.

" Now, isn't it ?" replied Lord Robert. He had finished the bread and butter.

Then he told her she was a dear, and he was glad something had suggested to Mr. Campion that he would have other views of living for this week.

" You are a joy, Robert! " she said, " but you will have to behave here. None of the tricks you played at Fotherington in October, my child. Aunt Katherine would put you in a corner. Miss Travers has been here a week, and can tell you I am truthful about it." " Indeed, *yes I"* I said.

" But I *must* know how you got here," she commanded.

Just then, fortunately, Malcolm, who had been hovering near, came up and joined us, and would talk too; but if he had been a table, or a chair, he could not have mattered less to Lord Robert! He is quite wonderful! He is not the least rude, only perfectly simple and direct, always getting just what he wants, with rather an appealing expression in his blue eyes. In a minute or two he and I were talking together, and Malcolm and Lady Verningham a few yards *off. I* felt so happy. He makes one like that, I don't know for what reason.

" Why did you look so stonily indifferent when I came up," he asked. " I was afraid you were annoyed with me for coming."

Then I told him about Lady Katherine, and my stupidly not having mentioned meeting him at Branches.

" Oh! then I stayed with Christopher after you leftII see," he said. " Had I met you in London ?"

" We won't tell any stories about it. They can think what they please."

" Very well! " he laughed. " I can see I shall have to manoeuvre a good deal to talk quietly to you here, but you will stand with me, won't you, out shooting to-morrow! "

I told him I did not suppose we should be allowed to go out, except perhaps for lunchI but he said he refused to believe in such cruelty.

Then he asked me a lot of things about how I had been getting on, and what I intended to do next. He has the most charming way of making one feel that one knows him very well, he looks at one every now and then straight in the eyes, with astonishing frankness. I have never seen any person so quite without airs, I don't suppose he is ever thinking a bit the effect he is producing. Nothing has two meanings with him like with Mr. Carruthers. If he had said I was to stay and marry him, I am sure he would have meant it, and I really believe I should have stayed!

"Do you remember our morning packing ?" he said, presently, in such a caressing voice. " I was so happy, weren't you? "

I said I was.

"And Christopher was mad with us! He was like a bear with a sore head after you left, and insisted upon going up to town on Monday just for the day; he came over here on Tuesday, didn't he ? "

" No, he did not," I was obliged to say, and I felt cross about it still, I don't know why.

" He is a queer creature," said Lord Robert, "and I am glad you have not seen him⎮I don't want him in the way. I am a selfish brute, you know."

I said Mrs. Carruthers had always brought me up to know men were that, so such a thing would not prejudice me against him.

He laughed. " You must help me to come and sit and talk again, after dinner," he said. " I can see the red-haired son means you for himself, but, of course, I shall not allow that!"

I became uppish.

" Malcolm and I are great friends," I said, demurely. " He walks me round the golf course in the park, and gives me advice."

" Confounded impertinence! " said Lord Robert.

" He thinks I ought not to go to Claridge's alone when I leave here, in case some one made love to me. He feels if I looked more like his sisters it would be safer. I have promised that Veronique shall stay at the other side of the door if I have visitors."

" Oh, he is afraid of that, is he! Well, I thinkitisvery probable his fears will be realized, as I shall be in London," said Lord Robert.

" But how do you know," I began, with a questioning, serious air; " how do you know I should listen ? You can't go on to deaf people, can you ?"

" Are you deaf?" he asked. " I don't think so, anyway I would try to cure your deafness." He bent close over to me, pretending to pick up a book.

Oh, I was having such a nice time!

All of a sudden I felt I was really living, the blood was jumping in my veins, and a number of provoking, agreeable things came to the tip of my tongue to say, and I said them. We were so happy!

Lord Robert is such a beautiful shape, that pleased me too; the perfect lines of things always give me a nice emotion. The other men look thick and clumsy beside him, and he does have such lovely clothes and ties!

We talked on and on. He began to show me he was deeply interested in me. His eyes, so blue and expressive, said even more than his words. I like to see him looking down ; his eyelashes are absurdly long and curly, not jet black like mine and Mr. Carruthers', but dark brown and soft, and shaded, and oh! I don't know how to say quite why they are so attractive. When one sees them half resting on his cheek it makes one feel it would be nice to put out the tip of one's finger, and touch them. I never spent such a delightful afternoon. Only alas! it was all too short.

"We will arrange to sit together after dinner," he whispered, as even before the dressing gong had rung Lady Katherine came and fussed about, and collected every one, and more or less drove them off to dress, saying, on the way upstairs, to me, that I need not come down if I had rather not!

I thanked her again, but remained firm in my intention of accustoming myself to company.

Stay in my room, indeed, with Lord Robert at dinner|never!

However, when I did come down, he was surrounded by Montgomeries, and pranced into the dining-room with Lady Verningham. She must have arranged that.

I had such a bore! A young Mackintosh cousin of Mary's husband, and on the other side the parson. The one talked about botany in a hoarse whisper, with a Scotch accent, and the other gobbled his food, and made kind of pious jokes in between the mouthfuls!

I said|when I had borne it bravely up to the ices|I hated knowing what flowers were composed of, I only liked to pick them. The youth stared, and did not speak much more. For the parson, " yes " now and then did, and like that we got through dinner.

Malcolm was opposite me, and he gaped most of the time. EVen he might have been better than the botanist, but I suppose Lady Katherine felt these two would be a kind of half mourning for me. No one could have felt gay with them.

After dinner Lady Verningham took me over to a sofa with her, in a corner. The sofas here don't have pillows, as at Branches, but fortunately this one is a little apart, though not comfortable, and we could talk.

" You poor child," she said, " you had a dull time. I was watching you! What did that MTavish creature find to say to you?"

I told her, and that his name was Mackintosh, not Mc Tavish.

" Yes, I know," she said, " but I call the whole clan M Tavish|it is near enough, and it does worry Mary so; she corrects me every time. Now don't you want to get married, and be just like Mary?" There was a twinkle in her eye.

I said I had not felt wild about it yet. I wanted to go and see life first.

But she told me one couldn't see life unless one was married.

" Not even if one is an adventuress, like me ? " I asked.

" A *what* "

" An adventuress," I said. " People do seem so astonished when I say that! I have got to be one, you know, because Mrs. Carruthers never left me the money after all, and in the book I read about it, it said you were that if you had nice clothes, and|and|red hair| and things and no home."

She rippled all over with laughter.

" You duck!" she said. " Now you and I will be friends. Only you must not play with Robert Vavasour. He belongs to me! He is one of my special and particular own pets. Is it a bargain ?"

I do wish now I had had the pluck then to say straight out that I rather liked Lord Robert, and would not make any bargain, but one is foolish sometimes when taken suddenly. It is then when I suppose it shows if one's head is screwed on firmly, and mine wasn't to-night. But she looked so charming, and I felt a little proud, and perhaps ashamed to show that I am very much interested in Lord Robert, especially if he belongs to her, whatever that means, and so I said it was a bargain, and of course I had never thought of playing with him, but when I came to reflect afterwards, that is a promise, I suppose, and I sha'n't be able to look at him any more under my eyelashes. And I don't know why I feel very wide awake and tired, and rather silly, and as if I wanted to cry tonight.

However, she was awfully kind to me, and lovely, and has asked me to go and stay with her, and lots of nice things, so it is all for the best, no doubt. But when Lord Robert came in, and came over to us, it did feel hard having to get up at once and go and pretend I wanted to talk to Malcolm.

I did not dare to look up often, but sometimes, and I found Lord Robert's eyes were fixed on me with an air of reproach and entreaty, and the last time there was wrath as well ?

Lady Verningham kept him with her until every one started to go to bed.

There had been music and bridge, and other boring diversions happening, but I sat still. And I don't know what Malcolm had been talking about, I had not been listening, though I kept murmuring " Yes " and " No."

He got more and more *empresse,* until suddenly I realized he was saying, as we rose:

" You have promised! Now remember, and I shall ask you to keep it|to-morrow! "

And there was such a loving, mawkish, wobbly look in his eyes, it made me feel quite sick. The horrible part is, I don't know what I have promised any more than the man in the moon ! It may be something perfectly dreadful, for all I know! Well, if it is a fearful thing, like kissing him, I shall have to break my word,|which I never do for any consideration whatever.

Oh, dear! oh, dear! it is not always so easy to laugh at life as I once thought! I almost wish I were settled down, and had not to be an adventuress. Some situations are so difficult. I think now I shall go to bed.

I wonder if Lord Robert|no, what is the good of wondering; he is no longer my affair.

I shall blow out the light!

8

SECTION 8

300, Park Street, *Saturday night, Nov.*

I Do not much care to look back to the rest of my stay at Tryland. It is an unpleasant memory.

That next day after I last wrote, it poured with rain, and every one came down cross to breakfast. The whole party appeared except Lady Verningham, and breakfast was just as stiff and boring as dinner. I happened to be seated when Lord Robert came in, and Malcolm was in the place beside me. Lord Robert hardly spoke, and looked at me once, or twice, with his eyebrows right up.

I did long to say it was because I had promised Lady Ver I would not play with him that I was not talking to him now like the afternoon before. I wonder if he ever guessed it. Oh! I wished then, and I have wished a hundred times since, that I had never promised at all. It seemed as if it would be wisest to avoid him, as how could I explain the change in myself. I hated the food, and Malcolm had such an air of proprietorship, it annoyed me as much as I could see it annoyed Lady Katherine. I sniffed at him, and was as disagreeable as could be.

The breakfasts there don't shine, and porridge is pressed upon people by Mr. Montgomerie. "Capital stuff to begin the day, Bur-r-r," he says.

Lord Robert could not find anything he wanted, it seemed. Every one was peevish. Lady Katherine has a way of marshalling people on every occasion ; she reminds me of a hen with chickens, putting her wings down, and clucking, and chasing, till they are all in a corner. And she is rather that shape, too, very much rounded in front. The female brood soon found themselves in the morning-room, with the door shut, and no doubt the male things fared the same with their host, anyway we saw no more of them till we caught sight of them passing the windows in 'scutums and mackintoshes, a depressed company of sportsmen.

The only fortunate part was that Malcolmhad found no opportunity to remind me of my promise, whatever it was, and I felt safer.

Oh ! that terrible morning! Much worse than when we were alonelnearly all of them labout seven women beyond the familyl began fancy work.

One, a Lady Letitia Smith, was doing a crewel silk blotting-book that made me quite bilious to look at, and she was very shortsighted, and had such an irritating habit of asking every one to match her threads for her. They knitted ties and stockings, and crocheted waistcoats and comforters and hoods for the North Sea fishermen, and one even tatted. Just like housemaids do in their spare hours to trim Heaven knows what garment of unbleached calico.

I asked her what it was for, and she said for the children's pinafores in her " Guild " work. If one doesn't call that waste of time, I wonder what is!

Mrs. Carruthers said it was much more useful to learn to sit still and not fidget than to fill the world with rubbish like this.

Mary Mackintosh dominated the conversation. She and Lady Letitia Smith, who have both small babies, revelled in nursery details, and then whispered bits for uslthe young girlslnot to hear. We caught scraps though, and it sounded gruesome, whatever it was about. Oh ! I do wonder when I get married if I shall grow like them.

I hope not.

It is no wonder married men are obliged to say gallant things to other people, if, when they get home, their wives are like that.

I tried to be agreeable to a lady who was next me. She was a Christian Scientist, and wore glasses. She endeavoured to convert me, but I was abnormally thick-headed that day, and had to have things explained over and over, so she gave it up at last.

Finally when I felt I should do something desperate, a footman came to say Lady Vern- ingham wished to see me in her room, and I bounded uplbut as I got to the door I saw them beginning to shake their heads over her.

" Sad that dear Ianthe has such irregular habits of breakfasting in her roomlso bad for her," etc., etc., but thank heaven, I was soon outside in the hall, where her maid was waiting for me.

One would hardly have recognized that it was a Montgomerie apartment, the big room overlooking the porch, where she was located. So changed did its aspect seem! She had numbers of photographs about, and the loveliest gold toilet things, and lots of frilled garments, and flowers, and scent bottles, and her own pillows propping her up, all blue silk, and lovely muslin embroideries, and she did look such a sweet cosy thing among it all. Her dark hair in fluffs round her face, and an angelic lace cap over it. She was smoking a cigarette, and writing numbers of letters with a gold stylograph pen. The blue silk quilt was strewn with correspondence, and newspapers, and telegraph forms. And her garment was low-necked, of course, and thin like mine are. I wondered what Alexander would have thought if he could have seen her in contrast to Mary! I know which I would choose if I were a man!

" Oh, there you are!" she exclaimed, looking up and puffing smoke clouds. " Sit on the bye-bye, Snake-girl. I felt I must rescue you from the horde of Holies below, and I wanted to look at you in the daylight. Yes, you have extraordinary hair, and real eyelashes and complexion, too. You are a witch thing, I can see, and we shall all have to beware of you! "

I smiled. She did not say it rudely, or I should have been uppish at once. She has a wonderful charm.

" You don't speak much, either," she continued. " I feel you are dangerous! that is why I am being so civil to you; I think it wisest. I can't stand girls as a rule! " And she went into one of her ripples of laughter. " Now say you will not hurt me! "

" I should not hurt anyone," I said, " unless they hurt me first|and I like you|you are so pretty."

" That is all right," she said, " then we are comrades. I was frightened about Robert last evening, because I am so attached to him, but you were a darling after dinner, and it will be all right now; I told him you would probably marry Malcolm Montgomerie, and he was not to interfere."

" I shall do nothing of the kind! " I exclaimed, moving off the bed. " I would as soon die|as spend the rest of my life here at|Tryland."

" He will be fabulously rich one day, you know, and you could get round Pere Montgomerie in a trice, and revolutionize the whole place. You had better think of it."

" I won't," I said, and I felt my eyes sparkle. She put up her hands as if to ward off an evil spirit, and she laughed again.

" Well, you sha'n't then! Only don't flash those emeralds at me, they give me quivers all over!"

" Would *you* like to marry Malcolm ?" I asked, and I sat down again. " Fancy being owned by that! Fancy seeing it every day! Fancy living with a person who never sees a joke from week's end to week's end. Oh! "

"As for that"|and she puffed smoke| " husbands are a race apart|there are men, women, and husbands, and if they pay bills, and shoot big game in Africa, it is all one ought to ask of them; to be able to see jokes is superfluous. Mine is most inconvenient, because he generally adores me, and at best only leaves me for a three weeks' cure at Homburg, and now and then a week in Paris, but Malcolm could be sent to the Rocky Mountains, and places like that, continuously; he is quite a sportsman."

" That is not my idea of a husband," I said.

"Well, what is your idea, Snake-girl?"

"Why do you call me 'Snake-girl?'" I asked. " I hate snakes."

She took her cigarette out of her mouth, and looked at me for some seconds.

" Because you are so sinuous, there is not a stiff line about your movements|you are utterly wicked looking and attractive too, and un-English, and what in the world Aunt Katherine asked you here for, with those hideous girls, I can't imagine. I would not have if my three angels were grown up, and like them." Then she showed me the photographs of her three angelslthey are pets.

But my looks seemed to bother her, for she went back to the subject.

" Where do you get them from ? Was your mother some other nation ?"

I told her how poor mamma had been rather an accident, and was nobody much. " One could not tell, you see, she might have had any quaint creature beyond the grandparents lperhaps I am mixed with Red Indian, or nigger."

She looked at me searchingly.

" No, you are not, you are Venetianlthat is itlsome wicked, beautiful friend of a Doge come to life again."

" I know I am wicked," I said ; " I am always told it, but I have not done anything yet, or had any fun out of it, and I do want to."

She laughed again.

" Well, you must come to London with me when I leave here on Saturday, and we will see what we can do."

This sounded so nice, and yet I had a feeling that I wanted to refuse; if there had been a tone of patronage in her voice, I would have in a minute. We sat and talked a long time, and she did tell me some interesting things. The world, she assured me, was a delightful place if one could escape bores, and had a good cook and a few friends. After a while I left her, as she suddenly thought she would come down to luncheon.

" I don't think it would be safe, at the present stage, to leave you alone with Robert," she said.

I was angry.

" I have promised not to play with him, is that not enough ! " I exclaimed.

" Do you know, I believe it is, Snake-girl! " she said, and there was something wistful in her eyes, " but you are twenty, and I am past thirty, andlhe is a man !lso one can't be too careful! " Then she laughed, and I left her putting a toe into a blue satin slipper, and ringing for her maid.

I don't think age can matter much, she is far far more attractive than any girl, and she need not pretend she is afraid of me. But the thing that struck me then, and has always struck me since is that to have to *hold* a man by one's own manoeuvres could not be agreeable to one's self-respect. I would *never* do that under any circumstances ; if he would not stay because it was the thing he wanted to do most in the world, he might go. I should say, *"Jem'enfiche!"*

At luncheon, for which the guns came in, lno nice picnic in a lodge as at BrancheslI purposely sat between two old gentlemen, and did my best to be respectful and intelligent. One was quite a nice old thing, and at the end began paying me compliments. He laughed, and laughed at everything I said. Opposite me were Malcolm and Lord Robert, with Lady Ver between them. They both looked sulky. It was quite a while before she could get them gay and pleasant. I did not enjoy myself.

After it was over, Lord Robert deliberately walked up to me.

" Why are you so capricious ?" he asked. " I won't be treated like this, you know very well I have only come here to see you. We are such friendslor were. Why ?"

Oh! I did want to say I was friends still, and would love to talk to him. He seemed so- adorably good looking, and such a shape! and his blue eyes had the nicest flash of anger in them.

I could have kept my promise to the letter, and yet broken it in the spirit, easily enough, by letting him understand by inferencelbut of course one could not be so mean as that, when one was going to eat her salt, so I looked out of the window, and answered coldly that I was quite friendly, and did not understand him, and I immediately turned to my old gentleman, and walked with him into the library. In fact I was as cool as I could be without being actually rude, but all the time there was a flat, heavy feeling round my heart. He looked so cross and reproachful, and I did not like him to think me capricious.

We did not see them again until tea; the sportsmen, I mean. But tea at Tryland is not

a friendly time. It is just as stiff as other meals. Lady Ver never let Lord Robert leave her side, and immediately after tea everybody who stayed in the drawing-room played bridge, where they were planted until the dressing-bell rang.

One would have thought Lady Katherine would have disapproved of cards, but I suppose every one must have one contradiction about them, for she loves bridge, and played for the lowest stakes with the air of a " needy adventurer " as the books say.

I can't write the whole details of the rest of the visit. I was miserable, and that is the truth. Fate seemed to be against Lord Robert speaking to meleven when he triedland I felt I must be extra cool and nasty because IlOh! well, I may as well say itlhe attracts me very much. I never once looked at him from under my eyelashes, and after the next day, he did not even try to have an explanation.

He glanced with wrath sometimeslespecially when Malcolm hung over meland Lady Ver said his temper was dreadful.

She was so sweet to me, it almost seemed as if she wanted to make up to me for not letting me play with Lord Robert.

(Of course I would not allow her to see I minded that.)

And finally Friday came, and the last night.

I sat in my room from tea until dinner. I could not stand Malcolm any longer. I had fenced with him rather well up to that, but that promise of mine hung over me. I nipped him every time he attempted to explain what it was, and to this moment I don't know, but it did not prevent him from saying tiresome, loving things, mixed with priggish advice. I don't know what would have happened only when he got really horribly affectionate just after tea I was so exasperated, I launched this bomb.

" I don't believe a word you are sayingl your real interest is Angela Grey."

He nearly had a fit, and shut up at once.

So, of course, it is not a horse. I felt sure of

it. Probably one of those people Mrs. Car-

ruthers said all young men knew; their adolescent measles and chicken-pox she called them.

All the old men talked a great deal to me; and even the other two young ones, but these last days I did not seem to have any of my usual spirits. Just as we were going to bed on Friday night Lord Robert came up to Lady Ver|she had her hand through my arm,

"I can come to the play with you to-morrow night, after all," he said. "I have wired to Campion to make a fourth, and you will get some other woman, won't you ? "

"I will try," said Lady Ver, and she looked right into his eyes, then she turned to me. " I shall feel so cruel leaving you alone, Evangeline" (at once almost she called me Evangeline, I should never do that with strangers)," but I suppose you ought not to be seen at a play just yet."

" I like being alone," I said. " I shall go to sleep early."

Then they settled to dine all together at her house, and go on; so, knowing I should seehim again, I did not even say good-bye to Lord Robert, and he left by the early train.

A number of the guests cameup to London with us.

My leavetaking with Lady Katherine had been coldly cordial. I thanked her deeply for her kindness in asking me there. She did not renew the invitation; I expect she felt a person like I am, who would have to look after herself, was not a suitable companion to her altar-cloth and poker workers.

Up to now|she told Lady Ver|of course I had been most carefully brought up and taken care of by Mrs. Carruthers, although she had not approved of her views. And having done her best for me at this juncture, saving me from staying alone with Mr. Carruthers, she felt it was all she was called upon to do. She thought my position would become too unconventional for their circle in future ! Lady Ver told me all this with great glee. She was sure it would amuse me, it so amused her|but it made me a teeny bit remember the story of the boys and the frogs!

Lady Ver now and then puts out a claw which scratches, while she ripples with laughter. Perhaps she does not mean it.

This house is nice, and full of pretty things as far as I have seen. We arrived just in time to fly into our clothes for dinner. I am in a wee room four stories up, by the three angels. I was down first, and Lord Robert and Mr. Campion were in the drawing-room. Sir Charles Verningham is in Paris, by the way, so I have not seen him yet.

Lord Robert was stroking the hair of the eldest angel, who had not gone to bed. The loveliest thing she is, and so polite, and different from Mary Mackintosh's infants.

He introduced Mr. Campion stiffly, and returned to Mildred|the angel.

Suddenly mischief came into me, the reaction from the last dull days, so I looked straight at Mr. Campion from under my eyelashes, and it had the effect it always has on people, he became interested at once. I don't know why this does something funny to them. I remember I first noticed it in the schoolroom at Branches. I was doing a horrible exercise upon the *Participe Passt,* and feeling very *Jgarde,* when one of the old Ambassadors came in to see Mademoiselle. I looked up quickly, with my head a little down, and he said to Mademoiselle, in a low voice, in German, that I had the strangest eyes he had ever seen, and that up look under the eyelashes was the affair of the devil!

Now I knew even then the afiair of the devil is something attractive, so I have never forgotten it, although I was only about fifteen at the time. I always determined I would try it when I grew up, and wanted to create emotions. Except Mr. Carruthers and Lord Robert I have never had much chance though.

Mr. Campion sat down beside me on a sofa, and began to say at once that I ought to be going to the play with them; I spoke in my velvet voice, and said I was in too deep mourning, and he apologized so nicely, rather confused.

He is quite a decent-looking person, smart and well-groomed, like Lord Robert, but not that lovely shape. We talked on for about ten minutes. I said very little, but he never took his eyes off my face. All the time I was conscious that Lord Robert was fidgeting and playing with a china cow that was on a table near, and just before the butler announced Mrs. Fairfax, he dropped it on the floor, and broke its tail off.

Mrs. Fairfax is not pretty; she has reddish gold hair, with brown roots, and a very dark skin, but it is nicely done|the hair, I mean, and perhaps the skin too, as sideways you can see the pink sticking up on it. It must be rather a nuisance to have to do all that, but it is certainly better than looking like Mary Mackintosh. She doesn't balance nicely, bits of her are too long, or too short. I do like to see everything in the right place|like Lord Robert's figure. Lady Ver came in just then, and we all went down to dinner. Mrs. Fairfax gushed at her a good deal. Lady Ver does not like her much, she told me in the train,but she was obliged to wire to her to come, as she could not get any one else Mr. Campion liked, on so short a notice.

" The kind of woman every one knows, and who has no sort of pride," she said.

Well, even when I am really an adventuress I sha'n't be like that.

Dinner was very gay.

Lady Ver, away from her decorous relations, is most amusing. She says anything that comes into her head. Mrs. Fairfax got cross because Mr. Campion would speak to me, but as I did not particularly take to her, I did not mind, and just amused myself. As the party was so small Lord Robert and I were obliged to talk a little, and once or twice I forgot, and let myself be natural and smile at him. His eyebrows went up in that questioning pathetic way he has, and he looked so attractive|that made me remember again, and instantly turn away. When we were coming into the hall, while Lady Ver and Mrs. Fairfax were up putting on their cloaks, Lord Robert came up close to me, and whispered:

" I *can't* understand you. There is some reason for your treating me like this, and I will find it out! Why are you so cruel, little wicked tiger cat! " and he pinched one of my fingers until I could have cried out.

That made me so angry.

" How dare you touch me! " I said. " It is because you know I have no one to take care of me that you presume like this! "

I felt my eyes blaze at him, but there was a lump in my throat, I would not have been hurt, if it had been anyone else|only angry |but he had been so respectful and gentle with me at Branches|and I had liked him so much. It seemed more cruel for him to be impertinent now.

His face fell, indeed, all the fierceness went out of it, and he looked intensely miserable.

" Oh! don't say that! " he said, in a choked voice. " I|oh! that is the one thing, you know is not true."

Mr. Campion, with his fur coat fastened, came up at that moment, saying gallant things, and insinuations that we must meet again, but I said good-night quietly, and came up the stairs without a word more to Lord Robert.

"Good-night, EVangeline, pet," Lady Ver said, when I met her on the drawing-room landing, coming down. " I do feel a wretch leaving you, but to-morrow I will really try and amuse you. You look very pale, child|the journey has tried you probably."

" Yes, I am tired," I tried to say in a natural voice, but the end word shook a little, and Lord Robert was just behind, having run up the stairs after me, so I fear he must have heard.

"Miss Travers|please|" he implored, but I walked on up the next flight, and Lady Ver put her hand on his arm, and drew him down with her, and as I got up to the fourth floor I heard the front door shut.

And now they are gone, and I am alone. My tiny room is comfortable, and the fire is burning brightly. I have a big arm-chair and books, and this, my journal, and all is cosy| only I feel so miserable.

I won't cry and be a silly coward.

9

SECTION 9

Why, of course it is amusing to be free. And I am *not* grieving over Mrs. Carruthers' death|only perhaps I am lonely, and I wish I were at the theatre. No, I don't|I|oh, the thing I do wish is that|that|*No,* I won't write it even.

Good-night, Journal!

300, Park Street,

Wednesday, November

Oh ! how silly to want the moon! but that is evidently what is the matter with me. Here I am in a comfortable house with a kind hostess, and no immediate want of money, and yet I am restless, and sometimes unhappy.

For the four days since I arrived Lady Ver has been so kind to me, taken the greatest pains to try and amuse me, and cheer me up. We have driven about in her electric brougham and shopped, and agreeable people have been to lunch each day, and I have had what I suppose is a *suctis*. At least she says so.

I am beginning to understand things better,and it seems one must have no real feelings, just as Mrs. Carruthers always told me, if one wants to enjoy life.

On two evenings Lady Ver has been out with numbers of regrets at leaving me behind, and I have gathered she has seen Lord Robert, but he has not been here|I am glad to say.

I am real friends with the angels, who are delightful people, and very well brought up. Lady Ver evidently knows much better about it than Mary Mackintosh, although she does not talk in that way.

I can't think what I am going to do next. I suppose soon this kind of drifting will seem quite natural, but at present the position galls me for some reason. I *hate* to think people are being kind out of charity. How very foolish of me, though!

Lady Merrenden is coming to lunch tomorrow. I am interested to see her, because Lord Robert said she was such a dear. I wonder what has become of him, that he has not been here!I wonder. No, I am *too* silly.

Lady Ver does not get up to breakfast, and I go into her room, and have mine on another little tray, and we talk, and she reads me bits out of her letters.

She seems to have a number of people in love with her!that must be nice.

" It keeps Charlie always devoted," she said, " because he realizes he owns what the other men want."

She says, too, that all male creatures are fighters by nature, they don't value things they obtain easily, and which are no trouble to keep. You must always make them realize you will be off like a snipe if they relax their efforts to please you for one moment.

Of course there are heaps of humdrum ways of living, where the husband is quite fond, but it does not make his heart beat, and Lady Ver says she couldn't stay on with a man whose heart she couldn't make beat when she wanted to.

I am curious to see Sir Charles.

They play bridge a good deal in the afternoon, and it amuses me a little to talk nicely

10

SECTION 10

to the man who is out for the moment, and make him not want to go back to the game. I am learning a number of things.

Night.

Mr. CARRUTHERScame to call this afternoon. He was the last person I expected to see when I went into the drawing-room after luncheon, to wait for Lady Ver. I had my outdoor things on, and a big black hat, which is rather becoming, I am glad to say.

" You here! " he exclaimed, as we shook hands.

" Yes, why not ? " I said.

He looked very self-contained, and reserved, I thought, as if he had not the least intention of letting himself go to display any interest. It instantly aroused in me an intention to change all that.

" Lady Verningham kindly asked me to spend a few days with her when we left Try- land," I said, demurely.

" Oh! you are staying here! Well, I was over at Tryland the day before yesterdayl an elaborate invitation from Lady Katherine to ' dine and sleep quietly,' which I only accepted as I thought I should see you."

" How good of you," I said, sweetly. "And did they not tell you I had gone with Lady Verningham ?"

" Nothing of the kind. They merely announced that you had departed for London, so I supposed it was your original design of Claridge's, and I intended going round there some time to find you."

Again I said it was so good of him, and I looked down.

He did not speak for a second or two, and I remained perfectly still.

" What are your plans ?" he asked abruptly.

" I have no plans "

" But you must have|that is ridiculous| you must have made some decision as to where you are going to live! "

" No, I assure you," I said, calmly, " when I leave here on Saturday, I shall just get into a cab, and think of some place for it to take me to, I suppose, as we turn down Park Lane."

He moved uneasily, and I glanced at him up from under my hat. I don't know why he does not attract me now as much as he did at first. There is something so cold and cynical about his face.

"Listen, EVangeline," he said at last. " Something must be settled for you|I cannot allow you to drift about like this. I am more or less your guardian|you know|you must feel that."

" I don't a bit," I said.

" You impossible little|witch! " he came closer.

" Yes, Lady Verningham says I am a witch, and a snake, and all sorts of bad attractive things, and I want to go somewhere where I shall be able to show these qualities ! England is dull|what do you think of Paris ? "

Oh! it did amuse me, launching forth these remarks. They would never come into my head for any one else !

He walked across the room and back. His face was disturbed.

" You shall not go to Paris|alone. How can you even suggest such a thing," he said.

I did not speak. He grew exasperated.

" Your father's people are all dead, you tell me, and you know nothing of your mother's relations, but who was she? What was her name ? Perhaps we could discover some kith and kin for you."

" My mother was called Miss Tonkins," I said.

" *Called* Miss Tonkins ? "

"Yes."

" Then it was not her name|what do you mean ?"

I hated these questions.

" I suppose it was her name. I never heard she had another."

" Tonkins," he said, " Tonkins ?" and he looked searchingly at me, with his monk of the Inquisition air.

I can be so irritating not telling people
things when I like, and it was quite a while
before he elicited the facts from me, which
Mrs. Carruthers had often hurled at my head|in moments of anger, that poor mamma's father had been Lord de Brandreth, and her mother Heaven knows who!

" So you see "|I ended with|" I haven't any relations, after all, have I ?"

He sat down upon the sofa.

"EVangeline, there is nothing for it, you must marry me," he said.

I sat down opposite him.

"Oh! you are funny!" I said. "You, a clever diplomat, to know so little of women. Who in the world would accept such an offer!" and I laughed, and laughed.

" What am I to do with you!" he exclaimed, angrily.

" Nothing! " I laughed still, and I looked at him with my " affair of the devil" look. He came over, and forcibly took my hand.

" Yes, you are a witch," he said. "A witch who casts spells, and destroys resolutions and judgements. I determined to forget you, and put you out of my life|you are most unsuitable to me, you know, but as soon as I see you I am filled with only one desire. I *must* have you for myself|I want to kiss you|to touch you. I want to prevent any other man from looking at you|do you hear me, Evangeline?"

" Yes, I hear," I said. " But it does not have any effect on me. You would be awful as a husband. Oh! I know all about them!" and I looked up. " I saw several sorts at Tryland, and Lady Verningham has told me of the rest; and I know you would be no earthly good in that *role*!"

He laughed, in spite of himself, but he still held my hand.

" Describe their types to me, that I may see which I should be," he said, with great seriousness.

"There is the Mackintosh kind|humble and ' titsy-pootsy,' and a sort of under nurse," I said.

" That is not my size, I fear."

" Then there is the Montgomerie, selfish and bullying, and near about money "

" But I am not Scotch."

" No|well, Lord Kestervin was English,and he fussed and worried, and looked out trains all the time."

" I shall have a groom of the chambers."

" And they were all casual and indifferent to their poor wives! and boresome, and bored!! And one told long stories, and one was stodgy, and one opened his wife's letters before she was down !"

"Tell me the attributes of a perfect husband, then, that I may learn them," he said.

" They have to pay all the bills."

" Well, I could do that."

" And they have not to interfere with one's movements. And one must be able to make their hearts beat."

" Well, you could do *that!"* and he bent nearer to me. I drew back.

" And they have to take long journeys to the Rocky Mountains for months together, with men friends."

" Certainly not!" he exclaimed.

" There, you see!" I said, " the most important part you don't agree to. There is no use talking further."

" Yes, there is! You have not said half enough|have they to make your heart beat, too?"

" You are hurting my hand."

He dropped it.

"Have they?"

" Lady Ver said no husband could do that |the fact of there being one kept your heart quite quiet, and often made you yawn|but she said it was not necessary, as long as you could make theirs, so that they would do all you asked."

" Then do women's hearts never beat|did she tell you?"

" Of course they beat! How simple you are for thirty years old. They beat constantly for|oh|for people who are not husbands."

" That is the result of your observations, is it? You are probably right, and I am a fool."

" Some one said at lunch yesterday that a beautiful lady in Paris had her heart beating for you," I said, looking at him again.

He changed|so very little, it was not a start, or a wince even|just enough for me to know he felt what I said.

" People are too kind," he said. " But we have got no nearer the point. When will you marry me?"

" I shall marry you|never, Mr. Carru- thers," I said, " unless I get into an old maid soon, and no one else asks me. Then if you go on your knees I may put out the tip of my finger, perhaps!" and I moved towards the door, making him a sweeping and polite curtsey.

He rushed after me.

" Evangeline!" he exclaimed, " I am not a violent man as a rule, indeed I am rather cool, but you would drive any one perfectly mad. Some day some one will strangle you| Witch!"

" Then I had better run away to save my neck," I said, laughing over my shoulder as I opened the door and ran up the stairs, and I peeped at him from the landing above. He had come out into the hall. " Goodbye," I called, and without waiting to see|Lady Ver he tramped down the stairs and away.

" Evangeline, what *have* you been doing ?" she asked, when I got into her room, where her maid was settling her veil before the glass, and trembling over it|Lady Ver is sometimes fractious with her, worse than I am with Veronique, far.

" EVangeline, you look naughtier than ever; confess at once."

" I have been as good as gold," I said.

" Then why are those two emeralds sparkling so, may one ask ?"

"They are sparkling with conscious virtue," I said, demurely.

" You have quarrelled with Mr. Carruthers. Go away, Welby! Stupid woman, can't you see it catches my nose?"

Welby retired meekly (after she is cross Lady Ver sends Welby to the theatre|Welby adores her).

" EVangeline, how dare you! I see it all. I gathered bits from Robert. You have quarrelled with the very man you must marry !"

" What does Lord Robert know about me?" I said. That made me angry.

"Nothing; he only said Mr. Carruthers admired you at Branches."

" Oh! "

" He is too attractive, Christopher! he is one of the ' married women's pets,' as Ada Fairfax says, and has never spoken to a girl before. You ought to be grateful we have let him look at you!Iminx!Iinstead of quarrelling, as I can see you have." She rippled with laughter, while she pretended to scold me.

" Surely I may be allowed that chastened diversion," I said, " I can't go to theatres! "

" Tell me about it," she commanded, tapping her foot.

But early in Mrs. Carruthers' days, I learnt that one is wiser when one keeps one's own affairs to oneselfIso I fenced a little, and laughed, and we went out to drive finally, without her being any the wiser. Going into the Park, we came upon a troop of the 3rd Life Guards, who had been escorting the King to open something, and there rode Lord Robert

11

SECTION 11

in his beautiful clothes, and a floating plume lhe did look so lovelyland *my* heart suddenly began to beat; I could feel it, and was ashamed, and it did not console me greatly to reflect that the emotion caused by a uniform is not confined to nursemaids.

Of course, it must have been the uniform, and the black horselLord Robert is nothing to me. But I hate to think that mamma's mother having been nobody, I should have inherited these common instincts.

300, Park Street,
Thursday, November 24.
Evening.

Lady Merrenden is so nicelone of those kind faces that even a tight fringe in a net does not spoil. She is tall and graceful, past fifty perhaps, and has an expression of Lord Robert about the eyes. At luncheon she was sweet to me at once, and did not look as if she thought I must be bad just because I have red hair, like elderly ladies do generally.

I felt I wanted to be good and nice directly.She did not allude to my desolate position, or say anything without tact, but she asked me to lunch, as if I had been a queen, and would honour her by accepting. For some reason I could see Lady Ver did not wish me to go, she made all sorts of excuses about wanting me herself, but also, for some reason, Lady Merrenden was determined I should, and finally settled it should be on Saturday, when Lady Ver is going down to Northumberland to her father's, and I am going|where ? Alas, as yet I know not.

When she had gone, Lady Ver said old people without dyed hair or bridge proclivities were tiresome, and she smoked three cigarettes, one after the other, as fast as she could. (Welby is going to the theatre again to-night!)

I said I thought Lady Merrenden was charming. She snapped my head off, for the first time, and then there was silence|but presently she began to talk, and fix herself in a most becoming way on the sofa|we were in her own sitting-room, a lovely place, all blue silk and French furniture, and attractive things. She said she had a cold, and must stay indoors. She had changed immediately into a tea-gown |but I could not hear any cough.

" Charlie has just wired he comes back tonight," she announced at length.

" How nice for you!" I sympathized. " You will be able to make his heart beat! "

" As a matter of fact it is extremely inconvenient, and I want you to be nice to him and amuse him, and take his attention *off* me, like a pet, EVangeline," she cooed|and then, " What a lovely afternoon for November! I wish I could go for a walk in the Park," she said.

I felt it would be cruel to tease her further, and so announced my intention of taking exercise in that way with the angels.

" Yes, it will do you good, dear child," she said, brightly, " and I will rest here, and take care of my cold."

" They have asked me to tea in the nursery," I said, " and I have accepted."

" Jewel of a Snake-girl! " she laughed|she is not thick.

" Do you know the Torquilstone history? " she said, just as I was going out of the door.

I came back|why, I can't imagine, but it interested me.

" Robert's brother|half-brother, I mean| the Duke, is a cripple, you know, and he is *toque* on one point, too|their blue blood. He will never marry, but he can cut Robert off with almost the bare tide if he displeases him."

" Yes," I said.

" Torquilstone's mother was one of the housemaids, the old Duke married her before he was twenty-one, and she fortunately joined her beery ancestors a year or so afterwards, and then, much later, he married Robert's mother, Lady Ethelrida Fitz Walter|there is sixteen years between them|Robert and Torquilstone, I mean."

" Then what is he *toque* about blue blood for, with a *tache* like that?" I asked.

"That is just it. He thinks it is such a disgrace, that even if he were not a humpback, he says he would never marry to transmit this stain to the future Torquilstones|and if Robert ever marries anyone without a pedigree enough to satisfy an Austrian prince, he will disown him, and leave every *sou* to charity."

" Poor Lord Robert!" I said, but I felt my cheeks burn.

" Yes, is it not tiresome for him ? So, of course, he cannot marry until his brother's death; there is almost no one in England suitable."

" It is not so sad after all," I said, " there is always the delicious *role* of the ' married woman's pet' open to him, isn't there?" and I laughed.

" Little cat! " but she wasn't angry.

" I told you I only scratched when I was scratched first," I said, as I went out of the room.

The angels had started for their walk, and Veronique had to come with me at first to find them. We were walking fast down the path beyond Stanhope Gate, seeing their blue velvet pelisses in the distance, when we met Mr. Carruthers.

He stopped, and turned with me.

" Evangeline, I was so angry with you yesterday," he said, " I very nearly left London, and abandoned you to your fate, but

now that I have seen you again " he

paused.

" You think Paris is a long way off! " I said innocently.

" What have they been telling you ?" he said, sternly, but he was not quite comfortable.

" They have been saying it is a fine November, and the Stock Exchange is no place to play in, and if it were not for bridge, they would all commit suicide! That is what we talk of at Park Street."

" You know very well what I mean. What have they been telling you about me ?"

" Nothing, except that there is a charming French lady, who adores you, and whom you are devoted to|and I am so sympathetic|I like French women, they put on their hats so nicely."

"What ridiculous gossip|I don't think Park Street is the place for you to stay. I thought you had more mind than to chatter like this."

" I suit myself to my company!" I laughed, and waited for Veronique, who had stopped respectfully behind|she came up reluctantly. She disapproves of all English unconvention- ality, but she feels it her duty to encourage Mr. Carruthers.

Should she run on, and stop the young ladies? she suggested, pointing to the angels in front.

"Yes, do," said Mr. Carruthers, and before I could prevent her, she was *off*.

Traitress! She was thinking of her own comfortable quarters at Branches, I know!

The sharp, fresh air, got into my head. I felt gay, and without care. I said heaps of things to Mr. Carruthers, just as I had once before to Malcolm, only this was much more fun, because Mr. Carruthers isn't a red-haired Scotchman, and can see things.

It seemed a day of meetings, for when we got down to the end, we encountered Lord Robert, walking leisurely in our direction. He looked as black as night when he caught sight of us.

" Hello, Bob!" said Mr. Carruthers, cheer, fully. "Ages since I saw you|will you come and dine to-night ? I have a box for this winter opera that is on, and I am trying to persuade Miss Travers to come. She says Lady Vern- ingham is not engaged to-night, she knows, and we might dine quietly, and all go, don't you think so ?"

Lord Robert said he would, but he added, " Miss Travers would never come out before; she said she was in too deep mourning." He seemed aggrieved.

" I am going to sit in the back of the box, and no one will see me," I said," and I do love music so."

" We had better let Lady Verningham know at once then," said Mr. Carruthers.

Lord Robert announced he was going there now, and would tell her.

I knew that! The blue tea-gown, with the pink roses, and the lace cap, and the bad cold were not for nothing. (I wish I had not written

12

SECTION 12

this, it is spiteful of me, and I am not spiteful as a rule. It must be the east wind.)

Thursday night, Nov.

" Now that you have embarked upon this," Lady Ver said, when I ventured into her sitting-room, hearing no voices, about six o'clock (Mr. Carruthers had left me at the door, at the end of our walk, and I had been with the angels at tea ever since), " Now that you have embarked upon this opera, I say, you will have to dine at Willis's with us. I won't be in when Charlie arrives from Paris. A windy day, like to-day, his temper is sure to be impossible."

" Very well," I said.

Of what use after all for an adventuress like me to have sensitive feelings.

" And I am leaving this house at a quarter to seven. I wish you to know, EVangeline, pet ! " she called after me, as I flew off to dress.

As a rule Lady Ver takes a good hour to make herself into the attractive darling she is in the evening I she has not to do much, because she is lovely by nature; but she potters, and squabbles with Welby, to divert herself, I suppose.

However, to-night, with the terror upon her of a husband fresh from a rough Channel passage, going to arrive at seven o'clock, she was actually dressed and down in the hall when I got there, punctually at 6.45, and in the twinkle of an eye we were rolling in the electric to Willis's. I have only been there once before, and that to lunch in Mrs. Car- ruthers" days with some of the Ambassadors, and it does feel gay going to a restaurant at night. I felt more excited than ever in my life, and such a situation, too.

Lord Robertl.*fruit dlfendul* and Mr. Car- ruthers *empress* and to be kept in bounds!

More than enough to fill the hands of a maiden of sixteen, fresh from a convent, as old Count Someroff used to say when he wanted to express a really difficult piece of work.

They were waiting for us just inside the door, and again I noticed that they were both lovely creatures, and both exceptionally distinguished looking.

Lady Ver nodded to a lot of people before we took our seats in a nice little corner. She must have an agreeable time with so many friends. She said something which sounds so true in one of our talks, and I thought of it then.

" It is wiser to marry the life you like, because, after a little, the man doesn't matter." She has evidently done thatlbut I wish it could be possible to have bothlthe Man and the Life!lWell! Well!

One has to sit rather close on those sofas, and as Lord Robert was not the host, he was put by me. The other two at a right angle to us.

I felt exquisitely gaylin spite of having an almost high black dress on, and not even any violets!

It was dreadfully difficult not to speak nicely to my neighbour, his directness and simplicity are so engaging, but I did try hard to concentrate myself on Christopher, and leave him alonelonly I don't know whylthe sense of his being so near me made me feelI don't quite know what. However, I hardly spoke to him, Lady Ver shall never say I did not play fair, though insensibly even she herself drew me into a friendly conversation, and then Lord Robert looked like a happy schoolboy.

We had a delightful time.

Mr. Carruthers is a perfect host. He has all the smooth and exquisite manners of the old diplomats, without their false teeth and things. I wish I were in love with himlor even I wish something inside me would only let me feel it was my duty to marry him ; but it jumps up at me every time I want to talk to myself about it, and says " Absolutely impossible."

When it came to starting for the opera, "Mr. Carruthers will take you in his brougham, EVangeline," Lady Ver said, " and I will be protected by Robert. Come along, Robert!" as he hesitated.

" Oh, I say, Lady Ver! " he said, " I would love to come with youlbut won't it look rather odd for Miss EVangeline to arrive alone with Christopher. Consider his character!"

Lady Ver darted a glance of flame at him, and got into the electric; while Christopher, without hesitation, handed me into his brougham. Lord Robert and I were two puppets, a part I do not like playing.

I was angry altogether. She would not have dared to have left me to go like this, if I had been any one who mattered. Mr. Carruthers got in, and tucked his sable rug round me. I never spoke a word for a long time, and Covent Garden is not far off, I told myself. I I can't say why I had a sense of *malaise.*

There was a strange look in his face, as a great lamp threw alight on it. "Evangeline," he said, in a voice I have not yet heard, " when are you going to finish playing with me|I am growing to love you, you know."

" I am very sorry to hear it," I said, gently. " I don't want you to|oh! please *don't* " as he took my hand. " I|I|if you only knew how I *hate* being touched!"

He leant back, and looked at me. There is something which goes to the head a little about being in a brougham with nice fur rugs, alone with some one at night. The lights flashing in at the windows, and that faint scent of a very good cigar. I felt fearfully excited. If it had been Lord Robert, I believe|well

He leant over very close to me. It seemed in another moment he would kiss me|and what could I do then|I couldn't scream, or jump out in Leicester Square, could I ?

" Why do you call me EVangeline?" I said, by way of putting him off. "I never said you might."

" Foolish child|I shall call you what I please. You drive me mad|I don't know what you were born for. Do you always have this effect on people?"

"What|effect?" I said,to gain time ;we had got nearly into Long Acre.

"An effect that causes one to lose all discretion. I feel I would give my soul to hold you in my arms."

I told him I did not think it was at all nice or respectful of him to talk so. That I found such love revolting.

" You tell me in your sane moments I am most unsuitable to you|you try to keep away from me, and then, when you get close, you begin to talk this stuff! I think it is an insult !" I said, angry and disdainful. " When I arouse devotion and tenderness in some one,then I shall listen, but to you and to this|never!"

" Go on!" he said. " Even in the dim light you look beautiful when cross."

" I am not cross," I answered. " Only absolutely disgusted."

By that time, thank goodness, we had got into the stream of carriages close to the Opera House. Mr. Carruthers, however, seemed hardly to notice this.

"Darling," he said, "I will try not to annoy you, but you are so fearfully provoking. I tell you truly, no man would find it easy to keep cool with you."

" Oh! I don't know what it is being coo) or not cool! " I said, wearily. " I am tired of every one, even as tiny a thing as Malcolm Montgomerie gets odd like this ! "

He leant back and laughed, and then said angrily,"Impertinence ! I will|wring|his-neck !"

" Thank heaven we have arrived! " I exclaimed, as we drove under the portico. I gave a great sigh of relief.

Really, men are very trying and tiresome, and if I shall always have to put up with these scenes through having red hair, I almost wish it were mouse coloured, like Cicely Parker's. Mrs. Carruthers often said, " You need not suppose, Evangeline, that you are going to have a quiet life with your colouring|the only thing one can hope for is that you will screw on your head."

Lady Ver and Lord Robert were already in the hall waiting for us, but the second I saw them I knew she had been saying something to Lord Robert, his face so gay and *debonnaire* all through dinner, now looked set and stern, and he took not the slightest notice of me as we walked to the box, the big one next the stage on the pit tier.

Lady Ver appeared triumphant; her eyes
were shining with big blacks in the middle,
and such bright spots of pink in her cheeks,
she looked lovely; and I can't think why,but I suddenly felt I hated her. It was
horrid of me, for she was so kind, and settled me in the corner behind the curtain,
where I could see and not be seen, rather far back, while she and Lord Robert were
quite in the front. It was " Carmen "lthe opera. I have never seen it before.

Music has such an effectlevery note seems to touch some emotion in me. I feel
wicked, or
good, or exalted, orlor Oh, some queer
feeling that I don't know what it isla kind of electric current down my back, and
as if, as if I would like to love some one, and have them to kiss me. Oh! it sounds
perfectly dreadful what I have writtenlbut I can't help itlthat is what some music does
to me, and I said always I should tell the truth here.

From the very beginning note to the end I was feelinglfeeling. Oh, how I understand
herlCarmen!l.*fruit difendu* attracted her solthe beautiful, wicked, fascinating snake. I
also wanted to dance, and to move like that, and I unconsciously quivered perhaps. I
was cold as ice, and fearfully excited. The backof Lord Robert's beautifully set head
impeded my view at times. How exquisitely groomed he is, and one could see at a
glance *his* mother had not been a housemaid. I never have seen anything look so well
bred as he does.

Lady Ver was talking to him in a cooing, low voice, after the first act, and the
second act, and indeed even when the third act had begun. He seemed much more *em-
pressi* with her than he generally does. Itlit hurt melthat and the music and the dancing,
and Mr. Carruthers whispering passionate little words at intervals, even though I paid
no attention to them, but altogether I, too, felt a kind of madness.

Suddenly Lord Robert turned round, and for five seconds looked at me. His lovely
expressive blue eyes, swimming with wrath and reproach, andloh, how it hurt me!l
contempt! Christopher was leaning over the back of my chair, quite close, in a devoted
attitude.

Lord Robert did not speak, but if a look could wither, I must have turned into a
deadoak leaf. It awoke some devil in me. What had / done to be annihilated so! /
was playing perfectly fairlkeeping my word to Lady Ver, and oh! I felt as if it were
breaking my heart.

But that look of Lord Robert's! It drove me to distraction, and every instinct to
be wicked and attractive that I possess came up in me. I leant over to Lady Ver, so
that I must be close to him, and I said little things to her, never one word to him, but
I moved my seat, making it certain the corner of his eye must catch sight of me, and
I allowed my shoulders to undulate the faintest bit to that Spanish music. Oh, I can
dance as Carmen too I Mrs. Carruthers had me taught every time we went to Paris,
she loved to see it herself.

I could hear Christopher breathing very quickly. "My God!" he whispered. "A
man would go to hell for you."

Lord Robert got up abruptly and went out of the box.

Then it was as if Don Jose's dagger plungedinto my heart, not Carmen's. That sounds high flown, but I mean itla sudden sick, cold sensation, as if everything was numb. Lady Ver turned round pettishly to Christopher. " What on earth is the matter with Robert ?" she said.

" There is a Persian proverb which asserts a devil slips in between two winds," said Christopher; " perhaps that is what has happened in this box to-night."

Lady Ver laughed harshly, and I sat there still as death. And all the time the music and the movement on the stage went on. I am glad she is murdered in the end,

glad ! Only I would like to have seen

the blood gush out. I am fierce|fierce| sometimes.

300, Park Street, *Friday morning, Nov. zth.*

I Know just the meaning of dust and ashes |for that is what I felt I had had for breakfast this morning, the day after " Carmen."

Lady Ver had given orders she was not to be disturbed, so I did not go near her, and crept down to the dining-room, quite forgetting the master of the house had arrived. There he was|a strange, tall, lean man with fair hair, and sad, cross, brown eyes, and a nose inclined to pink at the tip|a look of indigestion about him, I feel sure. He was sitting in front of a " Daily Telegraph " propped up on the tea-pot, and some cold, untasted sole on his plate.

I came forward. He looked very surprised.

"I|I'm Evangeline Travers,"I announced.

He said " How d'you do " awkwardly; one could see without a notion what that meant.

" I'm staying here," I continued. " Did you not know?"

" Then won't you have some breakfast| beastly cold, I fear," politeness forced him to utter. " No|lanthe never writes to me|I had not heard any news for a fortnight, and I have not seen her yet."

Manners have been drummed into me from early youth, so I said politely, "You only arrived from Paris late last night,did you not?"

" I got in about seven o'clock, I think," he replied.

" We had to leave so early, we were going to the Opera," I said.

" A Wagner that begins at unearthly hours, I suppose," he murmured absently.

" No, it was ' Carmen'|but we dined first with my|my|guardian, Mr. Carruthers."

" Oh."

We both ate for a little|the tea was greenish-black|and lukewarm|no wonder he has dyspepsia.

"Are the children in, I wonder," he hazarded, presently.

" Yes," I said. " I went to the nursery and saw them as I came down."

At that moment the three angels burst into the room, but came forward decorously, and embraced their parent. They did not seem to adore him like they do Lady Ver.

" Good morning, papa," said the eldest, and the other two repeated it in chorus. "We hope you have slept well, and had a nice passage across the sea."

They evidently had been drilled outside!

Then, nature getting uppermost, they patted him patronizingly.

" Daddie, darling, have you brought us any new dolls from Paris ?"

" And I want one with red hair, like Evan- geline," said Yseult, the youngest.

Sir Charles seemed bored and uncomfortable; he kissed his three exquisite bits of Dresden china, so like, and yet unlike himself|they have Lady Ver's complexion, but brown eyes and golden hair like him.

" Yes, ask Harbottle for the packages," he said. " I have no time to talk to you|tell your mother I will be in for lunch," and making excuse to me for leaving so abruptly|an appointment in the City|he shuffled out of the room.

I wonder how Lady Ver makes his heart beat. I *don't* wonder she prefers|Lord Robert.

" Why is papa's nose so red ?" said Yseult.

" Hush ! " implored Mildred. " Poor papa has come off the sea."

" I don't love papa," said Corisande, the middle one. " He's cross, and sometimes he makes darling mummie cry."

" We must always love papa," chanted Mildred, in a lesson voice. " We must always love our parents, and grandmamma, and grandpapa, and aunts and cousins|Amen." The "Amen" slipped out unawares, and she looked confused and corrected herself when she had said it.

" Let's find Harbottle. Harbottle is papa's valet," Corisande said, "and he is much thoughtfuller than papa. Last time he brought me a Highland boy doll, though papa had forgotten I asked for it."

They all three went out of the room, first kissing me, and curtseying sweetly when they got to the door. They are never rude, or boisterous | the three angels, I love them.

Left alone, I did feel like a dead fish. The
column " London Day by Day" caught my eye
in the " Daily Telegraph," and I idly glanced
down it|not taking in the sense of the words,until " The Duke of Torquilstone has arrived at Vavasour House, St. James's from abroad," I read.

Well, what did it matter to me; what did anything matter to me ? Lord Robert had met us in the hall again, as we were coming out of the Opera; he looked very pale, and he apologized to Lady Ver for his abrupt departure. He had got a chill, he said, and had gone to have a glass of brandy, and was all right now, and would we not come to supper, and various other *empresst* things, looking at her with the greatest devotion|I might not have existed.

She was capricious, as she sometimes is. " No, Robert, I am going home to bed. I have got a chill too," she said.

And the footman announcing the electric at that moment, we flew off", and left them. Christopher having fastened my sable collar with an air of possession, which would have irritated me beyond words at another time, but I felt cold and dead, and utterly numb.

Lady Ver did not speak a word on the way back, and kissed me frigidly as she went in to her room|then she called out:

" I am tired, Snake-girl|don't think I am cross|good-night! " and so I crept up to bed.

To-morrow is Saturday, and my visit ends. After my lunch with Lady Merrenden I am a wanderer on the face of the earth.

Where shall I wander to|I feel I want to go away by myself|away where I shall not see a human being who is English. I want to tor- get what they look like|I want to shut out of my sight their well-groomed heads|I want, oh, I do not know what I do want.

Shall I marry Mr. Carruthers ? He would eat me up, and then go back to Paris to the lady he loves|but I should have the life I like |and the Carruthers' emeralds are beautiful |and I love Branches|and|and

" Her ladyship would like to see you, Miss," said a footman.

So I went up the stairs.

Lady Ver was in a darkened room, soft pink blinds right down beyond the half-drawn blue silk curtains.

" I have a fearful head, EVangeline," she said.

" Then I will smooth your hair," and I climbed up beside her, and began to run over her forehead with the tips of my fingers.

" You are really a pet, Snake-girl," she said, " and you can't help it."

"I can't help what?"

" Being a witch. I knew you would hurt me, when I first saw you, and I tried to protect myself by being kind to you."

" Oh, dear Lady Ver!" I said, deeply moved. " I would not hurt you for the world, and indeed, you misjudge me; I have kept the bargain to the very letter and|spirit."

" Yes, I know you have to the letter, at least|but why did Robert go out of the box last night ? " she demanded, wearily.

" He said he had got a chill, did not he ?' I replied, lamely. She clasped her hands passionately.

"A chill!!! You don't know Robert! he never had a chill in his life," she said. " Oh, he is the dearest, dearest being in the world. He makes me believe in good and all things honest. He isn't vicious, he isn't a prig, and he knows the world, and he lives in its ways like the rest of us, and yet he doesn't begin by thinking every woman is fair game, and undermining what little self-respect she may have left to her."

" Yes." I said. I found nothing else to say.

" If I had had a husband like that I would never have yawned," she went on, " and, besides, Robert is too masterful, and would be too jealous to let one divert oneself with another."

" Yes," I said again, and continued to smooth her forehead.

" He has sentiment, too|he is not matter- of-fact and brutal|and oh, you should see him on a horse, he is too, too beautiful! " She stretched out her arms in a movement of weariness that was pathetic, and touched me.

" You have known him a long, long time ?" I said, gently.

" Perhaps five years, but only casually until

this season. I was busy with some one else

before. I have played with so many." Then she

roused herself up. " But Robert is the only|one who has never made love to me. Always dear and sweet and treating me like a queen, as if I were too high for that, and having his own way, and not caring a pin for any one's opinion. And I have wanted him to make love to me often. But now I realize it is no use. Only you sha'n't have him, Snake-girl! I told him as we were going to the Opera you were as cold as ice, and were playing with Christopher, and I am going to take him down to Northumberland with me to-morrow out of your way. He shall be my devoted friend at any rate. You would break his heart, and I shall still hold you to your promise."

I said nothing.

" Do you hear, I say *you* would break his heart. He would be only capable of loving straight to the end. The kind of love any other woman would die for, but youIyou are Carmen."

At all events not *she,* nor any other woman, shall ever see what I am, or am not. My heart is not for them to peck at. So I said, calmly:

" Carmen was stabbed."

" And serve her right! Fascinating, fiendish demon!" Then she laughed, her mood changing.

" Did you see Charlie? " she said.

" We breakfasted together."

" Cheerful person, isn't he ? "

" No," I said. " He looked cross and ill."

" Ill! " she said, with a shade of anxiety. " Oh, you only mean dyspeptic."

" Perhaps."

" Well, he always does when he comes from Paris. If you could go into his room, and see the row of photographs on his mantelpiece, you might guess why."

" Pictures of' Sole Dieppoise' and ' Poulet Victoria aux truffes,' no doubt," I hazarded.

She doubled up with laughter. " Yes, just that! " she said. "Well, he adores me in his way, and will bring me a new Cartier ring to make up for itIyou will see at luncheon."

" He is a perfect husband, then?"

" About the same as you will find Christopher. Only Christopher will start by being an exquisite lover, there is nothing he does not know, and Charlie has not an idea of that part. Heavens! the dullness of my honeymoon !"

" Mrs. Carruthers said all honeymoons were only another parallel to going to the dentist, or being photographed. Necessary evils to be got through for the sake of the results."

" The results!"

" Yes; the nice house, and the jewels, and the other things."

" Oh 1 Yes, I suppose she was right, but if one had married Robert one would have had both." She did not say both what, but oh! I knew.

" You think Mr. Carruthers will make a fair husband, then?" I asked.

" You will never really know Christopher. I have been acquainted with him for years. You will never feel he would tell you the whole truth about anything. He is an epicure and an analyst of sensations; I don't know if he has any gods, he does not believe in them if he has, he believes in no one, and nothing, but perhaps himself. He is violently in love with you for the moment, and he wants to marry you because he cannot obtain you on any other terms."

" You are flattering," I said, rather hurt.

" I am truthful. You will probably have a delightful time with him, and keep him devoted to you for years, because you are not in love with him, and he will take good care you do not look at any one else. I can imagine if one were in love with Christopher he would break one's heart, as he has broken poor Alicia Verney's."

" Oh, but how silly! people don't have broken hearts now; you are talking like out of a book, dear Lady Ver."

" There are a few cases ol broken hearts, but they are not for book reasonslof death and tragedy, etc.; they are because we cannot have what we want, or keep what we have," and she sighed.

We did not speak for a few minutes, then she said quite gaily,

" You have made my head better, your touch is extraordinary; in spite of all I like you, Snake-girl. You are not found on every gooseberry bush."

We kissed lightly, and I left her and went to my room.

Yes, the best thing I can do is to marry Christopher; I care for him so little that the lady in Paris won't matter to me, even if she is like Sir Charles's Poulet a la Victoria aux truffes. He is such a gentleman, he will at least be kind to me and refined and considerate; and the Carruthers' emeralds are divine, and just my stones. I shall have them reset by Cartier. The lace, too, will suit me, and the sables, and I shall have the suite that Mrs. Carruthers used at Branches done up with pale green, and burn all the Early Victorians. And no doubt existence will be full of triumphs and pleasure.

But oh! I wish, I wish it were possible to obtain "both."

300, Park Street, *Friday night.*

Luncheon passed off very well. Sir Charles returned from the City improved in temper, and, as Lady Ver had predicted, presented her with a Cartier jewel. It was a brooch, not a ring, but she was delighted, and purred to him.

He was a little late and we were seated, a party of eight, when he came in. They all chaffed him about Paris, and he took it quite good-humouredly|he even seemed pleased. He has no wit, but he looks like a gentleman, and I daresay as husbands go he is suitable.

I am getting quite at home in the world, and can talk to any one. I listen and I do not talk much, only when I want to say something that makes them think.

A very nice man sat next me to-day, he reminded me of the old generals at Branches. We had quite a war of wits, and it stimulated me.

He told me, among other things, when he discovered who I was, that he had known papa|papa was in the same Guards with him |and that he was the best-looking man of his day. Numbers of women were in love with him, he said, but he was a faithless being and rode away.

" He probably enjoyed himself, don't you think so ? and he had the good luck to die in his zenith," I said.

" He was once engaged to Lady Merrenden, you know. She was Lady Sophia Vavasour then, and absolutely devoted to him, but Mrs. Carruthers came between them and carried him off; she was years older than he was, too, and as clever as paint."

" Poor papa seems to have been a weak creature, I fear."

" All men are weak," he said.

" And then he married and left Mrs. Carruthers, I suppose ?" I asked. I wanted to hear as much as I could.

" Yeslels," said my old Colonel. " I was best man at the wedding "

" And what was she like, my mamma?"

" She was the loveliest creature I ever saw," he said; " as lovely as you, only you are the image of your father, all but the hair, his was fair."

" No one has ever said I was lovely before. Oh! I am so glad if you think so," I said. It did please me. I have often been told I am attractive and extraordinary, and wonderful, and divinelbut never just lovely. He would not say any more about my parents, except they hadn't a *sou* to live on, and were not very happy; Mrs. Carruthers took care of that.

Then, as every one was going, he said: " I am awfully glad to have met youlwe must be pals, for the sake of old times," and he gave me his card for me to keep his address, and told me if ever I wanted a friend to send him a line, Colonel Tom Garden, The Albany.

I promised I would.

" You might give me away at my wedding," I said, gaily. " I am thinking of getting married, some day! "

" That I will," he promised," and, by Jove, the man will be a fortunate fellow."

Lady Ver and I drove after luncheonlwe paid some calls, and went in to tea with the Montgomeries, who had just arrived at Brown's Hotel for a week's shopping.

" Aunt Katherine brings those poor girls up always at this time, and takes them to some impossible old dressmaker of her own, in the day, and to Shakespeare, or a concert, at night, and returns with them equipped in more hideous garments each year. It is positively cruel," said Lady Ver, as we went up the stairs to their *appartement.*

There they were, sitting round the tea-table, just as at Tryland. Kirstie and Jean embroidering and knitting, and the other two reading new catalogues of books for their work !!!

Lady Ver began to tease them. She asked them all sorts of questions about their new frocks, and suggested they had better go to Paris, once in a way. Lady Katherine was like ice. She strongly disapproved of my being with her niece, one could see.

The connection with the family, she hoped, would be ended with my visit to Tryland. Malcolm was arriving in town, too, we gathered, and Lady Ver left a message to ask him to dine to-night.

Then we got away.

" If one of those lumps of suet had a spark of spirit, it would go straight to the devil," Lady Ver said, as we went down the stairs. " Think of it! ties and altar-cloths in London ! Mercifully they could not dine tonight. I had to ask them, and they generally come once while they are uplthe four girls and Aunt Katherineland it is with the greatest difficulty I can collect four young men for them if they get the least hint who they are to meet. I generally secure a couple of socially budding Jews, because I feel the subscriptions for their charities, which they will pester whoever they do sit next for, are better filched from the Hebrew, than from some pretty needy guardsman. Oh, what a life! "

She was so kind to me on the way back;

she said she hated leaving me alone on the
morrow, and that I must settle now what I was
going to do, or she would not go.   I said Iwould go to Claridge's where Mrs.
Carruthers and I had always stayed, and remain perfectly quietly alone with Veronique.
I could afford it for a week.   So we drove there, and made the arrangement.

" It is absolutely impossible for you to go on like this, dear child," she said.   " You
must have a chaperon; you are far too pretty to stay alone in a hotel.   What *can* I do
for you ?"

I felt so horribly uncomfortable, I was really at my wits' end.   Oh! it is no fun
being an adventuress, after all, if you want to keep your friends of the world as well.

" Perhaps it won't matter if I don't see any one for a few days," I said.   " I will
write to Paris; my old Mademoiselle is married there to a flourishing poet, I believe;
perhaps she would take me as a paying guest for a little."

" That is very visionaryIa French poet!   horrible, long-haired, frowsy creature.
Impossible ! Surely you see how necessary it is for you to marry Christopher as soon
as you can, Evangeline, don't you ?" she said, and I was obliged to admit there were
reasons.

" The truth is, you can't be the least eccentric, or unconventional, if you are good-
looking and unmarried," she continued; "you may snap your fingers at Society, but if
you do, you won't have a good time, and all the men will either foolishly champion
you, or be impertinent to you."

" Oh, I realize it," I said, and there was a lump in my throat.

" I shall write to Christopher to-morrow," she went on, " and thank him for our
outing last night, and I shall say something nice about you, and your loneliness, and
that he, as a kind of relation, may go and see you on Sunday, as long as he doesn't
make love to you, and he can take you to the ZooIdon't see him in your sitting-room.
That will give him just the extra fillip, and he will go, and you will be demure, and
then, by those stimulating lions' and tigers' cages, you can plight your troth. It will be
quite respectable. Wire to me at once on Monday, to Sedgwick, and you must come
back to Park Street directly I return on Thursday, if it is all settled."

I thanked her as well as I could.   She was quite ingenuous, and quite sincere.   I
should be a welcome guest as Christopher's *fiancte,* and there was no use my feeling
bitter about itIshe was quite right.

As I put my hand on Malcolm's skinny arm going down to the dining-room, the
only consolation was my fate has not got to be him! I would rather be anything in the
world than married to that!

I tried to be agreeable to Sir Charles. We were only a party of six. An old Miss
Har- penden, who goes everywhere to play bridge, and Malcolm, and one of Lady
Ver's young men, and me. Sir Charles is absent, and brings himself back; he fiddles
with the knives and forks, and sprawls on the table rather, too. He looks at Lady Ver
with admiration in his eyes. It is true then, in the intervals of Paris, I suppose, she can
make his heart beat.

Malcolm made love to me after dinner.   We were left to talk when the others sat
down to bridge in the little drawing-room.

" I missed you so terribly, Miss Travers," he said, priggishly, " when you left us, that I realized I was extremely attracted by you."

" No, you don't say so!" I said, innocently. " Could one believe a thing like that."

"Yes," he said, earnestly. "You may indeed believe it."

" Do not say it so suddenly, then," I said, turning my head away, so that he could not see how I was laughing. "You see, to a red- haired person like me these compliments go to my head."

" Oh, I do not want to flurry you," he said, aifably. " I know I have been a good deal sought after|perhaps on account of my possessions" (this with arrogant modesty), "but I am willing to lay everything at your feet if you will marry me."

" EVerything!" I asked.

" Yes, everything."

" You are too good, Mr. Montgomerie| but what would your mother say ?"

He looked uneasy, and slightly unnerved.

" My mother, I fear, has old-fashioned notions|but I am sure if you went to her dressmaker|you|you would look different."

" Should you like me to look different then |you wouldn't recognize me, you know, if I went to her dressmaker."

" I like you just as you are," he said, with an air of great condescension.

" I am overcome," I said, humbly; " but| but|what is this story I hear about Miss Angela Grey ? A lady, I see in the papers, who dances at|the Gaiety, is it not ? Are you sure she will permit you to make this declaration without her knowledge?"

He became petrified.

"Who has told you about her?" he asked.

" No one," I said. " Jean said your father was angry with you on account of a horse of that name, but I chanced to see it in the list of attractions at the Gaiety|so I conclude it is not a horse, and if you are engaged to her, I don't think it is quite right of you to try and break my heart."

. '" Oh, Evangeline|Miss Travers "|he

spluttered. " I am greatly attached to you|the other was only a pastime|aloh! we men you know|young and|and|run after |have our temptations you know. You must think nothing about it. I will never see her again, except just finally to say good-bye. I promise you."

" Oh! I could not do a mean thing like that, Mr. Montgomerie," I said. " You must not think of behaving so on my account|I am not altogether heartbroken, you know|in fact I rather think of getting married myself."

He bounded up.

"Oh ! you have deceived me then ! "he said, in self-righteous wrath. " After all I said to you that evening at Tryland, and what you promised then! Yes, you have grossly deceived me."

I could not say I had not listened to a word he had said that night, and was utterly unconscious of what I had promised. Even his self- appreciation did not deserve such a blow as this! so I softened my voice, and natural anger at his words, and said quite gently,

" Do not be angry. If I have unconsciously

given you a wrong impression, I am sorry, but if one came to talking of deceiving, you have deceived me about Miss Grey, so do not let us speak further upon the matter. We are quits. Now, won't you be friends, as you have always been "land I put out my hand, and smiled frankly in his face. The mean little lines in it relaxedlhe pulled himself together and took my hand, and pressed it warmly. From which I knew there was more in the affair of Angela Grey than met the eye.

" EVangeline," he said. " I shall always love you, but Miss Grey is an estimable young woman, there is not a word to be said against her moral characterland I have promised her my hand in marriagelso perhaps we had better say good-bye."

" Good-bye," I said, " but I consider I have every reason to feel insulted by your offer, which was not, judging from your subsequent remarks, worth a moment's thought!"

" Oh, but I love you!" he said, and by his face, for the time, this was probably true. So I did not say any more, and we rose and joined the bridge players. And I contrived that he should not speak to me again alone before he said good-night.

" Did Malcolm propose to you," Lady Ver asked, as we came up to bed. " I thought I saw a look in his eye at dinner."

I told her he had done it in a kind of way, with a reservation in favour of Miss Angela Grey.

" That is too dreadful!" she said. " There is a regular epidemic in some of the Guards' regiments just now to marry these poor common things with high moral characters, andl indifferent feet! but I should have thought the cuteness of the Scot would have protected Malcolm from their designs. Poor Aunt Katherine!"

13

SECTION 13

Cla Ridge's, *Saturday, Nov. z6th.*

Lady Ver went off early to the station, to catch her train to Northumberland this morning, and I hardly saw her to say goodbye. She seemed out of temper too, on getting a note, she did not tell me whom it was from, or what it was about|only she said immediately after, that I was not to be stupid. " Do not play with Christopher further," she said, " or you will lose him. He will certainly go and see you to-morrow|he wrote to me this morning in answer to mine of last night| but he says he won't go to the Zoo|so you will have to see him in your sitting-room after all|he will come about four."

I did not speak.

" EVangeline," she said, " promise me you won't be a fool "

" I|won't be a fool," I said.

Then she kissed me, and was off, and a few moments after I also started for Claridge's.

I have a very nice little suite right up at the top, and if only it were respectable for me, and I could afford it, I could live here very comfortably by myself for a long time.

At a quarter to two I was ringing the bell at 200, Carl ton House Terrace, Lady Merren- den's House|with a strange feeling of excitement and interest. Of course it must have been because once she had been engaged to papa. In the second thoughts take to flash I remembered Lord Robert's words when I talked of coming to London alone at Branches; how he would bring me here, and how she would be kind to me until I could " hunt round."

Oh! it came to me with a sudden stab. He was leaning over Lady Ver in the northern train by now.

Such a stately beautiful hall it is|when the doors open|with a fine staircase going each way, and full of splendid pictures, and the whole atmosphere pervaded with an air of refinement and calm.

The footmen are tall, and not too young, and even at this time of the year have powdered hair.

Lady Merrenden was upstairs in the small drawing-room, and she rose to meet me, a book in her hand, when I was announced.

Her manners are so beautiful in her own home; gracious, and not the least patronizing.

" I am so glad to see you," she said. " I hope you won't be bored, but I have not asked any one to meet you|only my nephew, Tor- quilstone, is coming|he is a great sufferer, poor fellow, and numbers of faces worry him, at times."

I said I was delighted to see her alone. No look more kind could be expressed in a human countenance than is expressed in hers. She has the same exceptional appearance of breeding that Lord Robert has, tiny ears, and wrists, and head|even dressed as a charwoman, Lady Merrenden would look like a great lady.

Very soon we were talking without the least restraint; she did not speak of people, or of very deep things, but it gave one the impression of an elevated mind, and a knowledge of books, and wide thoughts. Oh ! I could love her so easily.

We had been talking for nearly a quarter of an hour|she had incidentally asked me where I was staying now, and had not seemed surprised or shocked when I said Claridge's, and by myself.

All she said was: "What a lonely little girl! but I daresay it is very restful sometimes to be by oneself, only you must let your friends come and see you, won't you."

" I don't think I have any friends," I said. " You see I have been out so little|but if you would come and see me|oh! I should be so grateful."

" Then you must count me as one of your rare friends! " she said.

Nothing could be so rare, or so sweet, as her smile. Fancy papa throwing over this angel for Mrs. Carruthers!! Men are certainly unaccountable creatures.

I said I would be too honoured to have her for a friend|and she took my hand.

" You bring back the long ago," she said. " My name is EVangeline, too. Sophia EVangeline|and I sometimes think you may have been called so in remembrance of me."

What a strange, powerful factor Love must be! Here these two women, Mrs. Carruthers and Lady Merrenden|the very opposites of each other|had evidently both adored papa, and both, according to their natures, had taken an interest in me, in consequence, the child of a third woman, who had superseded them both! Papa must have been extraordinarily fascinating for, to the day of her death, Mrs. Carruthers had his miniature on her table, with a fresh rose beside it|his memory the only soft spot, it seemed, in her hard heart.

And this sweet lady's eyes melted in tenderness when she spoke of the long agoIalthough she does not know me well enough yet to say anything further. To me papa's picture is nothing so very wonderful, just a good-looking young guardsman, with eyes shaped like mine, only gray, and light curly hair. He must have had "a way with him " as the servants say.

At that moment the Duke of Torquilstone came in. Oh, such a sad sight!

A poor hump-backed man, with a strong face and head, and a soured, suspicious, cynical expression. He would evidently have been very tall, but for his deformity, a hump stands out on his back, almost like Mr. Punch. He can't be much over forty, but he looks far older, his hair is quite gray.

Not a line, or an expression in him reminded me of Lord Robert, I am glad to say.

Lady Merrenden introduced us, and Lord Merrenden came in then, too, and we all went down to luncheon.

It was a rather small table, so we were all near one another, and could talk.

The dining-room is immense.

" I always have this little table when we are such a small party," Lady Merrenden said. " It is more cosy, and one does not feel so isolated."

How I agreed with her.

The Duke looked at me searchingly often, with his shrewd little eyes. One could not say if it was with approval, or disapproval.

Lord Merrenden talked about politics, and the questions of the day, he has a courteous manner, and all their voices are soft and refined. And nothing could have been more smooth and silent than the service.

The luncheon was very simple, and very good, but not half the numbers of rich dishes like at Branches, or Lady Ver's.

There was only one bowl of violets on the table, but the bowl was gold, and a beautiful shape, and the violets nearly as big as pansies. My eyes wandered to the picturesIGainsborough's, and Reynolds', and Romney'sIof stately men and women.

" You met my other nephew, Lord Robert, did you not?" Lady Merrenden said, presently. " He told me he had gone to Branches, where I believe you lived."

" Yes," I said, and oh ! it is too humiliating to write, I felt my cheeks get crimson at the mention of Lord Robert's name. What could she have thought? Can anything be so young ladylike and ridiculous.

" He came to the Opera with us the night before last," I continued. " Mr. Carruthers had a box, and Lady Verningham and I went with them." Then recollecting how odd this must sound in my deep mourning, I added, " I am so fond of music."

" So is Robert," she said. " I am sure he must have been pleased to meet a kindred spirit there."

Sweet, charming, kind lady! If she only knew what emotions were really agitating us in that box that nightII fear the actual love of music was the least of them !

The Duke, during this conversation, and from the beginning mention of Lord Robert's name, never took his eyes off my faceIit was very disconcerting; his look was clearer now, and it was certainly disapproving.

We had coffee upstairs, out of such exquisite Dresden cups, and then Lord Merrenden showed me some miniatures. Finally it happened that the Duke and I were left alone for a minute looking out of a window on to the Mall.

His eyes pierced me through and through |well at all events my nose and my ears and my wrists are as fine as Lady Merrenden's|poor mamma's odd mother does not show in me on the outside|thank goodness. He did not say much, only commonplaces about the view. I felt afraid of him, and rather depressed. I am sure he dislikes me.

" May I not drive you somewhere ?" my kind hostess asked. " Or, if you have nowhere in particular to go, will you come with me ?"

I said I should be delighted. An ache ot loneliness was creeping over me. I wanted to put off as long as possible getting back to the hotel. I wanted to distract my thoughts from dwelling upon to-morrow, and what I was going to say to Christopher. To-morrow that seems the end of the world.

She has beautiful horses, Lady Merrenden, and the whole turn-out, except she herself, is as smart as can be. She really looks a little frumpish out of doors, and perhaps that is why papa went on to Mrs. Carruthers. Goodness and dearness like this do not suit male creatures as well as caprice, it seems.

She was so good to me, and talked in the nicest way. I quite forgot I was a homeless wanderer, and arrived at Claridge's about half past four in almost good spirits.

" You won't forget I am to be one of your friends," Lady Merrenden said, as I bid her good-bye.

" Indeed I won't," I replied, and she drove *off*, smiling at me.

I do wonder what she will think of my marriage with Christopher.

Now it is night|I have had a miserable, lonely dinner in my sitting-room, Veronique has been most gracious and coddling|she feels Mr. Carruthers in the air, I suppose,|and so I must go to bed.

Oh ! why am I not happy, and why don't I think this is a delightful and unusual situation, as I once would have done. I only feel depressed and miserable, and as if I wished Christopher at the bottom of the sea. I have told myself how good-looking he is|and how he attracted me at Branches|but that was before|yes, I may as well write what I was going to|before Lord Robert arrived. Well, he and Lady Ver are talking together on a

14

SECTION 14

nice sofa by now, I suppose, in a big, well-lit drawing-room, and|oh !|I wish, I *wish* I had never made any bargain with her|perhaps now in that case|ah well

Sunday ajtermion.

No! I can't bear it. All the morning I have been in a fever, first hot and then cold. What will it be like. Oh ! I shall faint when he kisses me. And I know he will be dreadful like that, I have seen it in his eye|he will eat me up. Oh ! I am sure I shall hate it. No man has ever kissed me in my life, and I can't

judge, but I am sure it is frighful, unless I

feel as if I shall go crazy if I stay here any longer. I can't, I can't stop and wait, and face it. I must have some air first. There is a misty fog. I would like to go out and get lost in it, and I *will* too! Not get lost, perhaps, but go out in it, and alone. I won't have even Veronique. I shall go by myself into the Park. It is growing nearly dark, though only three o'clock. I have got an hour. It looks mysterious, and will soothe me, and

15

SECTION 15

---

suit my mood, and then, when I come in again, I shall perhaps be able to bear it bravely, kisses and all.

Clari Doe's,
Sunday evening, November 2"Jtk.

I have a great deal to writeland yet it is only a few hours since I shut up this book, and replaced the key on my bracelet.

By a quarter past three I was making my way through Grosvenor Square. Everything was misty and blurred, but not actually a thick fog, or any chance of being lost. By the time I got into the Park it had lifted a little. It seemed close and warm, and as I went on I got more depressed. I have never been out alone before ; that in itself seemed strange, and ought to have amused me.

The image of Christopher kept floating in front of me, his face seemed to have the expression of a satyr. Well, at all events, he would never be able to break my heart like " Alicia Verney's "Inothing could ever make me care for him. I tried to think of all the good I was going to get out of the affair, and how really fond I am of Branches.

I walked very fast, people loomed at me, and then disappeared in the mist. It was getting almost dusk, and suddenly I felt tired, and sat down on a bench.

I had wandered into a side path where there were no chairs. On the bench before mine I I saw, as I passed, a tramp huddled up. I wondered what his thoughts were, and if he felt any more miserable than I did. I daresay I was crouching in a depressed position too.

Not many people went by, and every moment it grew darker. In all my life, even on the days when Mrs. Carruthers taunted me about mamma being nobody, I have never felt so wretched. Tears kept rising in my eyes, and I did not even worry to blink them away. Who would see meland who in the world would care if they did see.

Suddenly I was conscious that a very perfect figure was coming out of the mist towards me, but not until he was close to me, and stopping with a start peered into my face, did I recognize it was Lord Robert.

" Evangeline ! " he exclaimed, in a voice of consternation. " Ilwhat, oh, what is the matter ?"

No wonder he was surprised. Why he had not taken me for some tramp too, and passed on, I don't know.

" Nothing," I said, as well as I could, and tried to tilt my hat over my eyes. I had no veil on unfortunately.

" I have just been for a walk. Why do you call me Evangeline, and why are you not in Northumberland ?"

He looked so tall and beautiful, and his face had no expression of contempt or anger now, only distress and sympathy.

" I was suddenly put on guard yesterday, and could not get leave," he said, not answering the first part. " But, oh, I can't bear to see you sitting here alone, and looking so, so miserable. Mayn't I take you home ? You will catch cold in the damp."

" Oh no, not yet. I won't go back yet! " I said, hardly realizing what I was saying. He sat down beside me, and slipped his hand into my muff, pressing my clasped fingerslthe gentlest, friendliest caress, a child might have made in sympathy. It touched some foolish chord in my nature, some want of self-control inherited from mamma's ordinary mother, I suppose, anyway the tears poured down my facell could not help it. Oh, the shame of it! to sit crying in the Park, in front of Lord Robert, of all people in the world, too!

" Dear, dear little girl," he said. " Tell me about it," and he held my hand in my muff with his strong warm hand.

" Ill have nothing to tell," I said, choking down a sob. " I am ashamed for you to see me like this, onlyII am feeling so very miserable."

" Dear child," he said. " Well, you are not to bell won't have it. Has some one been unkind to youltell me, tell me," his voice was trembling with distress.

"It'slit's nothing," I mumbled.

I dared not look at him, I knew his eyebrows would be up in that way that attracts me so dreadfully.

" Listen," he whispered almost, and bent over me. " I want you to be friends with me so that I can help you. I want you to go back to the time we packed your books together. God knows what has come between us sincel it is not of my doinglbut I want to take care of you, dear little girl to-day. Itloh, it hurts me so to see you crying here."

" I would like to be friends," I said. " I never wanted to be anything else, but I could not help it and I can't now."

" Won't you tell me the reason ?" he pleaded. " You have made me so dreadfully unhappy about it. I thought all sorts of things. You know I am a jealous beast."

There can't in the world be another voice as engaging as Lord Robert's, and he has a trick of pronouncing words that is too attractive, and the way his mouth goes when he is speaking, showing his perfectly chiselled lips under the little moustache! There is no use pretending ! I was sitting there on the bench going through thrills of emotion, and longing for him to take me in his arms. It is too frightful to think of! I must be bad after all.

" Now you are going to tell me everything about it," he commanded. " To begin with, what made you suddenly change at Tryland after the first afternoon, and then what is it that makes you so unhappy now ? "

" I can't tell you either," I said very low. I hoped the common grandmother would not take me as far as doing mean tricks to Lady Ver!

" Oh, you have made me wild!" he exclaimed, letting go my hand, and leaning both elbows on his knees, while he pushed his hat to the back of his head. " Perfectly mad with fury and jealousy. That brute Malcolm ! and then looking at Campion at dinner, and worst of all, Christopher in the box at ' Carmen!' Wicked, naughty little thing! And yet underneath I have a feeling it is for some absurd reason, and not for sheer devilment. If I thought that, I would soon get not to care. I did think it at ' Carmen.' "

" Yes, I know," I said.

" You know what ?" he looked up, startled; then he took my hand again, and sat close to me.

"Oh, please, please don't, Lord Robert!" I said.

It really made me quiver so with the loveliest feeling I have ever known, that I knew I should never be able to keep my head if he went on.

" Please, please, don't hold my hand," I said. " It it makes me not able to behave nicely."

" Darling," he whispered, " then it shows that you like me, and I sha'n't let go until you tell me every little bit."

" Oh, I can't, I can't! " I felt too tortured, and yet waves of joy were rushing over me. That *is* a word, " darling," for giving feelings down the back!

"EVangeline," he said, quite sternly, "will you answer this question then do you like me, or do you hate me ? Because, as you must know very well, I love you."

Oh, the wild joy of hearing him say that! What in the world did anything else matter! For a moment there was a singing in my ears, and I forgot everything but our two selves. Then the picture of Christopher waiting for me, with his cold, cynic's face and eyes blazing with passion, rushed into my vision, and the Duke's critical, suspicious, disapproving scrutiny, and I felt as if a cry of pain, like a wounded animal, escaped me.

" Darling, darling, what is it ? Did I hurt your dear little hand ?" Lord Robert exclaimed tenderly.

"No," I whispered, brokenly; "but I cannot listen to you. I am going back to Claridge's now, and I am going to marry Mr. Carruthers."

He dropped my hand as if it stung him.

" Good God! Then it is true," was all he said.

In fear I glanced at him|his face looked gray in the quickly gathering mist.

" Oh, Robert! " I said in anguish, unable to help myself. " It isn't because I want to. I|I|oh ! probably I love you|but I must, there is nothing else to be done."

" Isn't there! " he said, all the life and joy|coming back to his face. " Do you think I will let Christopher, or any other man in the world, have you now you have confessed that!!" and fortunately there was no one in sight| because he put his arms round my neck, and drew me close, and kissed my lips.

Oh, what nonsense people talk of heaven! sitting on clouds and singing psalms and things like that! There can't be any heaven half so lovely as being kissed by Robert|I felt quite giddy with happiness for several exquisite seconds, then I woke up. It was all absolutely impossible, I knew, and I must keep my head.

"Now you belong to me," he said, letting his arm slip down to my waist; " so you must begin at the beginning, and tell me everything."

" No, no," I said, struggling feebly to free myself, and feeling so glad he held me tight! " It is impossible all the same, and that only makes it harder. Christopher is coming to see me at four, and I promised Lady Ver I would not be a fool, and would marry him."

" A fig for Lady Ver," he said, calmly, " if|that is all; you leave her to me|she never argues with me! "

"It is not only that|I|I promised I would never play with you "

" And you certainly never shall," he said, and I could see a look in his eye as he purposely misconstrued my words, and then he deliberately kissed me again. Oh! I like it better than anything else in the world! How could any one keep their head with Robert quite close, making love like that ?

" You certainly never|never|shall," he said again, with a kiss between each word. "I will take care of that! Your time of playing with people is over, Mademoiselle! When you are married to me, I shall fight with any one who dares to look at you! "

" But I shall never be married to you, Robert," I said, though, as I could only be happy for such a few moments, I did not think it necessary to move away out of his arms. How thankful I was to the fog! and no one passing! I shall always adore fogs.

"Yes, you will," he announced, with perfeet certainty; " in about a fortnight, I should think. I can't and won't have you staying at Claridge's by yourself. I shall take you back this afternoon to Aunt Sophia. Only all that we can settle presently. Now, for the moment, I want you to tell me you love me, and that you are sorry for being such a little brute all this time."

" I did not know it until just now|but I think|I probably do love you|Robert! " I said.

He was holding my hand in my muff again, the other arm round my waist. Absolutely disgraceful behaviour in the Park; we might have been Susan Jane and Thomas Augustus, and yet I was perfectly happy, and felt it was the only natural way to sit.

A figure appeared in the distance|we started apart.

" Oh! really, really," I gasped, " we|you |must be different."

He leant back and laughed.

" You sweet darling! Well, come, we will go for a drive in a hansom|we will choose one without a light inside. Albert Gate is quite close, come!" and he rose, and taking my arm, not offering his to me, like in books, he drew me on down the path.

I am sure any one would be terribly shocked to read what I have written, but not so much if they knew Robert, and how utterly adorable he is. And how masterful, and simple, and direct! He does not split straws, or bandy words. I had made the admission that I loved him, and that was enough to go upon!

As we walked alone I tried to tell him it was impossible, that I must go back to Christopher, that Lady Ver would think I had broken my word about it. I did not, of course, tell him of her bargain with me over him, but he probably guessed that, because before we got into the hansom even, he had begun to put me through a searching cross-examination as to the reasons for my behaviour at Tryland, and Park Street, and the Opera. I felt like a child with a strong man, and every moment more idiotically happy, and in love with him.

He told the cabman to drive to Hammersmith, and then put his arm round my waist again, and held my hand, pulling my glove *off* backwards first. It is a great big granny muff of sable I have, Mrs. Carruthers' present on my last birthday. I never thought then to what charming use it would be put!

" Now I think we have demolished all your silly little reasons for making me miserable," he said. "What others have you to bring forward as to why you can't marry me in a fortnight?" -

I was silent|I did not know how to say it |the principal reason of all.

"EVangeline|darling," he pleaded. "Oh, why will you make us both unhappy|tell me at least."

" Your brother, the Duke," I said, very low. " He will never consent to your marrying a person like me with no relations."

He was silent for a second,|then, " My
brother is an awfully good fellow," he said,
" but his mind is warped by his infirmity.
You must not think hardly of him|he will|love you directly he sees you, like everyone else."

" I saw him yesterday," I said.
Robert was so astonished.
"Where did you see him?" he asked.

Then I told him about meeting Lady Mer- renden, and her asking me to luncheon, and about her having been in love with papa, and about the Duke having looked me through and through with an expression of dislike.

"Oh, I see it all!" said Robert, holding me closer. " Aunt Sophia and- I are great friends, you know, she has always been like my mother, who died when I was a baby. I told her all about you when I came from Branches, and how I had fallen deeply in love with you at first sight, and that she must help me to see you at|Tryland; and she did, and then I thought you had grown to dislike me, so when I came back she guessed I was unhappy about something, and this is her first step to find out how she can do me a good turn|oh! she is a dear!"

" Yes, indeed she is,1' I said.

" Of course she is extra interested in you if she was in love with your father! So that is all right, darling, she must know all about your family, and can tell Torquilstone. Why, we have nothing to fear!"

"Oh yes we have!" I said. "I know all the story of what your brother is *toqut* about. Lady Ver told me. You see the awkward part is, mamma was really nobody, her father and mother forgot to get married, and although mamma was lovely, and had been beautifully brought up by two old ladies at Brighton, it was a disgrace for papa marrying her|Mrs. Carruthers has often taunted me with this!"

"Darling!" he interrupted, and began to kiss me again, and that gave me such feelings I could not collect my thoughts to go on with what I was saying for a few minutes. We both were rather silly|if it is silly to be madly, wildly happy,|and oblivious of every thing else.

" I will go straight to Aunt Sophia now, when I take you back to Claridge's," he said, presently, when we had got a little calmer.

I wonder what kisses do that they make one have that perfectly lovely sensation down the back, just like certain music does, only much, much more so. I thought they would be dreadful things when it was a question of Christopher, but Robert! Oh well, as I said before, I can't think of any other heaven.

" What time is it ?" I had sense enough to ask presently.

He lit a match, and looked at his watch.

" Ten minutes past five," he exclaimed.

" And Christopher was coming about four," I said, " and if you had not chanced to meet me in the Park, by now I should have been engaged to him, and probably trying to bear his kissing me."

"My God!" said Robert, fiercely, "it makes me rave to think of it," and he held me so tight for a moment, I could hardly breathe.

" You won't have anyone else's kisses ever again, in this world, and that I tell you," he said, through his teeth.

"I|I don't want them," I whispered, creeping closer to him ; " and I never have had any, never any one but you, Robert."

" Darling," he said, "how that pleases me!"

Of course, if I wanted to, I could go on writing pages and pages of all the lovely things we said to one another, but it would sound, even to read to myself, such nonsense, that I can't, and I couldn't make the tone of Robert's voice, or the exquisite fascination of his ways |tender, and adoring, and masterful. It must all stay in my heart; but oh! it is as if a fairy with a wand had passed, and said " bloom " to a winter tree. Numbers of emotions that I had never dreamed about were surging through me|the flood-gates of everything in my soul seemed opening in one rush of love and joy- While we were together, nothing appeared to matter|all barriers melted away.

Fate would be sure to be kind to lovers like us!

We got back to Claridge's about six, and Robert would not let me go up to my sitting- room, until he had found out if Christopher had gone.

Yes, he had come at four, we discovered, and had waited twenty minutes, and then left, saying he would come again at half-past six.

" Then you will write him a note, and give it to the porter for him, saying you are engaged to me, and can't see him," Robert said.

" No, I can't do that|I am not engaged to you, and cannot be until your family consent, and are nice to me," I said.

" Darling," he faltered, and his voice trembled with emotion, "darling, love is between you and me, it is our lives|however that can go, the ways of my family, nothing shall ever separate you from me, or me from you, I swear it.   Write to Christopher."

I sat down at a table in the hall and wrote,

" Dear Mr. Carruthers,|I am sorry I was out," then I bit the end of my pen. " Don't come and see me this evening. I will tell you why in a day or two.

"Yours sincerely,

" Evangeline Travers."

" Will that do?" I said, and I handed it to Robert, while I addressed the envelope.

16

SECTION 16

" Yes," he said, and waited while I sealed it up, and gave it to the porter. Then, with a surreptitious squeeze of the hand, he left me to go to Lady Merrenden.

I have come up to my little sitting-room a changed being. The whole world revolves for me upon another axis, and all within the space of three short hours.

Cla Ridge's,

Sun day night, Nov. Jh.

Late this evening, about eight o'clock, when I had re-locked my journal, I got a note from Robert. I was just going to begin my dinner.

I tore it open, inside was another, I did not wait to look from whom, I was too eager to read his. I paste it in.

" Carlton House Terrace. " My Darling,|I have had a long talk with Aunt Sophia, and she is everything that is sweet and kind, but she fears Torquilstone will be a little difficult (*7 don't care, nothing* shall separate us now). She asks me not to go and see you again to-night, as she thinks it would be better for you that I should not go to the Hotel so late. Darling, read her note, and you will she how nice she is. I shall come round to-morrow, the moment the beastly stables are finished, about 12 o'clock. Oh! take care of yourself! What a difference tonight and last night! I was feeling horribly miserable and recklessland to-night! Well, you can guess! I am not half good enough for you, darling, beautiful Queenlbut I think I shall know how to make you happy. I love you!

" Good night my own,

" Robert."

" Do please send me a tiny line by my servantlI have told him to wait."

I have never had a love letter before. What lovely things they are! I felt thrills of delight over bits of it! Of course I see now that I must have been dreadfully in love with Robert all along, only I did not know it quite! I fell into a kind of blissful dream, and then I roused myself up to read Lady Merrenden's. I sha'n't put hers in too, it fills up too much, and I can't shut the clasp of my journallit is aperfectly sweet little letter, just saying Robert had told her the news, and that she was prepared to welcome me as her dearest niece, and to do all she could for us. She hoped I would not think her very tiresome and old fashioned suggesting Robert had better not see me again to-night, and if it would not inconvenience me, she would herself come round to-morrow morning, and discuss what was best to be done.

Veronique said Lord Robert's valet was waiting outside the door, so I flew to my table, and began to write. My hand trembled so I made a blot, and had to tear that sheet up, then I wrote another. Just a little word. I was frightened, I couldn't say loving things in a letter, I had not even spoken many to himl yet.

" I loved your note," I began, " and I think Lady Merrenden is quite right. I will be here at twelve, and very pleased to see you." I wanted to say I loved him, and thought twelve o'clock a long way off, but of course one could not write such things as thatlso I ended with just " Love from Evanoeline."

Then I read it over, and it did sound " missish " and sillylhowever, with the man waiting there in the passage, and Veronique fussing in and out of my bedroom, besides the waiters bringing up my dinner, I could not go tearing up sheets, and writing others, it looked so flurried, so it was put into an envelope. Then, in one of the seconds I was alone, I nipped ofF a violet from a bunch on the table, and pushed it in too. I wonder if he will think it sentimental of me! When I had written the name, I had not an idea where to address it. His was written from Carlton House Terrace, but he was evidently not there now, as his servant had brought it. I felt so nervous and excited, it was too ridiculouslI am very calm as a rule. I called the man, and asked him where was his lordship now? I did not like to say I was ignorant of where he lived.

" His lordship is at Vavasour House, Madame," he said, respectfully, but with the faintest shade of surprise that I should not know. " His lordship dines at home this evening with his grace."

I scribbled a note to Lady MerrendenlI would be delighted to see her in the morning at whatever time suited her. I would not go out at all, and I thanked her. It was much easier to write sweet things to her than to Robert.

When I was alone I could not eat. Veron- ique came in to try and persuade me. I looked so very pale, she said, she feared I had taken cold. She was in one of her "old mother" moods, when she drops the third person sometimes, and calls me " *man enfant.*"

" Oh, Veronique, I have not got a cold, I am only wildly happy ! " I said.

" Mademoiselle is doubtless *fiancee* to Mr. Carruthers. *Oh! man enfant adoree"* she cried, " *que je suis contents I "*

" Gracious no !" I exclaimed. This brought me back to Christopher with a start. What would he say when he heard ?

" No, Veronique, to some one much nicer| Lord Robert Vavasour."

Veronique was frightfully interested|Mr. Carruthers she would have preferred for me she admitted, as being more solid|more *rangl |plus a la fin de ses bStises,* but, no doubt, " Milor " was charming too, and for certain one day Mademoiselle would be Duchesse. In the meanwhile what kind of coronet would Mademoiselle have on her trousseau ?

I was obliged to explain that I should not have any|or any trousseau for an indefinite time, as nothing was settled yet. This damped her a little.

" *Un frere de Due, et pas de couronne!"* After seven years in England she was yet unable to understand these strange habitudes, she said.

She insisted upon putting me to bed directly after dinner|" to be prettier for Milor *de- main "* and then, when she had tucked me up, and was turning out the light in the centre of the room she looked back|" Mademoiselle is too beautiful like that," she said, as if it slipped from her|" *Man Dieu ! ilne s'embeterai pas, le Monsieur!"*

I WONDE

I wonder I wonder, I be obdurate strength c to spoil r.

Such a s |since I v what made clock of 1

Oh, now frightfully to keep nv the remark men. Figl never feel difficult to and simple haps beinu all the male terest will

worried, and I won't have to be tiresome myself. I hope so, because I really do love him so extremely, I would like to let myself go and be as sweet as I want to.

I am doing all the things I thought perfectly silly to hear of before. I kissed his letter, and slept with it on the pillow beside me, and this morning woke at six and turned on the electric light to read it again! The part where the " Darling" comes is quite blurry I see in daylight; that is where I kissed most I know!

I seem to be numb to everything else. Whether Lady Ver is angry or not does not bother me. I did play fair. She could not expect me to go on pretending when Robert had said straight out he loved me. But I am sure she will be angry, though, and probably rather spiteful about it.

I will write her the simple truth in a day or two, when we see how things go. She will guess by Robert not going to Sedgwick.

mercies). Then the old man opened a door, and without announcing my name, merely, "The lady, your grace," he held the door, and then went out and closed it softly.

It was a huge room splendidly panelled with dark carved *boiserie* Louis XV, the most beautiful of its kind I had ever seen, only it was so dimly lit with the same sort of shaded lamps one could hardly see into the corners.

The Duke was crouching in a chair, he looked fearfully pale and ill, and had an inscrutable expression on his face. Fancy a man so old-looking, and crippled, being even Robert's half-brother!

I came forward; he rose with difficulty, and this is the conversation we had.

" Please don't get up," I said, " if I may sit down opposite you."

" Excuse my want of politeness," he replied, pointing to a chair, " but my back is causing me great pain to-day."

He looked such a poor miserable, soured, unhappy creature, I could not help being touched.

" Oh, I am so sorry! " I said. " If I had known you were ill, I would not have troubled you now."

" Justice had better not wait," he answered, with a whimsical, cynical, sour smile. " State your case."

Then he suddenly turned on an electric lamp near me, which made a blaze of light in my face. I did not jump. I am glad to say I have pretty good nerves.

" My case is this: to begin with, I love your brother better than anything else in the world "

" Possibly: a number of women have done so," he interrupted. " Well ?"

" And he loves me," I continued, not noticing the interruption.

" Agreed. It is a situation that happens every day among young fools. You have known one another about a month, I believe ? "

" Under four weeks," I corrected.

He laughed bitterly.

" It cannot be of such vital importance to you then in that short time ! "

"It is of vital importance to me, and you know your brother's character; you will be able to judge as well as I if, or not, it is a matter of vital importance to him."

He frowned. " Well, your case."

" First, to demand on what grounds you condemned me as a ' devilish beauty ?' and why you assume that I should not be faithful to Robert for a year ? "

" I am rather a good judge of character," he said.

" You cannot be or you would see that whatever accident makes me have this objectionable outside, the me that lives within is an honest person who never breaks her word."

" I can only see red hair and green eyes, and a general look of the devil."

" Would you wish people always to judge by appearances then ?" I said. " Because, if so, I see before me a prejudiced, narrow-minded, cruel-tempered, cynical man, jealous of youth's joys. But /would not be so unjust as to stamp you with these qualities because of that! "

He looked straight at me, startled. " I may be all those things," he said. " You are probably right!"

" Then, oh, please don't be! " I went on quickly. " I want you to be kind to us. We, oh, we do, do so wish to be happy, and we are both so young, and life will be so utterly blank and worthless for all these years to the end if you part us now."

" I did not say I would part you," he said, '" coldly. " I merely said I refused to give Robert any allowance, and I shall leave everything in my power away from the title. If you like to get married on those terms you are welcome to."

Then I told him I loved Robert far too much to like the thought of spoiling his future.

" We came into each other's lives," I said. " We did not ask it of Fate, she pushed us there; and I tried not to speak to him because I had promised a friend of mine I would not, as she said she liked him herself, and it made us both dreadfully unhappy, and every day we mattered more to one another; until yesterday|when I thought he had gone away for good, and I was too miserable for words|we met in the Park, and it was no use pretending any longer. Oh ! you *can't* want to crush out all joy and life for us, just because I have red hair! It is so horribly unjust."

" You beautiful siren," he said. " You are coaxing me. How you know how to use your charms and your powers; and what *man* could resist your tempting face! "

I rose in passionate scorn.

" How dare you say such things to me! " I said. " I would not stoop to coax you|I will not again ask you for any boon! I only wanted you to do me the justice of realizing you had made a mistake in my character|to do your brother the justice of conceding the point that he has some right to love whom he chooses. But keep your low thoughts to yourself! Evil, cruel man! Robert and I have got something that is better than all your lands and money|a dear, great love, and I am glad; glad that he will not in the future receive anything that is in your gift. I shall give him the gift of myself, and we shall do very well without you," and I walked to the door, leaving him huddled in the chair.

Thus ended our talk on justice !

Never has my head been so up in the air. I am sure had Cleopatra been dragged to Rome in Augustus's triumph she would not have walked with more pride and contempt than I through the hall of Vavasour House.

The old servant was waiting for me, and Veronique, and the brougham.

" Call a hansom, if you please," I said, and stood there like a statue while one of the footmen had to run into St. James's Street for it.

Then we drove away, and I felt my teeth chatter, while my cheeks burnt. Oh! what an end to my scheme, and my dreams of perhaps success!

But what a beast of a man! What a cruel, warped, miserable creature. I will not let him separate me from Robert, never, never! He is not worth it. I will wait for him|my darling land, if he really loves me, some day we can be happy, and if he does not|but oh! I need not fear.

17

SECTION 17

I am still shaking with passion, and shall go to bed. I do not want any dinner.

Tuesday morning, Nov. 2)tA.

Veronique would not let me go to bed, she insisted upon my eating, and then after dinner I sat in an old, but lovely wrap of white crepe, and she brushed out my hair for more than an hour|there is such a tremendous lot of it, it takes time.

I sat in front of the sitting-room fire, and tried not to think. One does feel a wreck after a scene like that. At about half past nine I heard noises in the passage of people, and with only a preliminary tap Robert and Lady Merrenden came into the room. I started up, and Veronique dropped the brush, in her astonishment, and then left us alone.

Both their eyes were shining, and excited,
and Robert looked crazy with joy; he seized
me in his arms and kissed me, and kissed me,
while Lady Merrenden said, " You darling,EVangeline, you plucky, clever girl, tell us all about it! "

" About what! " I said, as soon as I could speak.

" How you managed it."

" Oh, I must kiss her first, Aunt Sophia! " said Robert. " Did you ever see anything so divinely lovely as she looks with her hair all floating like this|and it is all mine|every bit of it!!!"

"Yes, it is," I said sadly. "And that is about all of value you will get! "

" Come and sit down," said Robert, " Evangeline, you darling|and look at this ! "

Upon which he drew from his pocket a note. I saw at once it was the Duke's writing, and I shivered with excitement. He held it before my eyes.

" Dear Robert," it began, "I have seen her. I am conquered. She will make a magnificent Duchess. Bring her to lunch to-morrow. Yours, Torquilstone."

I really felt so intensely moved I could not speak.

" Oh, tell us, dear child, how did it happen| and what did you do|and where did you meet ?" said Lady Merrenden.

Robert held my hand.

Then I tried to tell them as well as I could, and they listened breathlessly. " I was very rude, I fear," I ended with, "but I was so angry."

"It is glorious," said Robert. "But the best part is that you intended to give me yourself with no prospect of riches. Oh, darling, that is the best gift of all."

" Was it disgustingly selfish of me ?" I said. " But when I saw your poor brother so unhappy looking, and soured, and unkind, with all his grandeur, I felt that to us, who know what love means, to be together was the thing that matters most in all the world."

Lady Merrenden then said she knew some people staying here who had an *appartement* on the first floor, and she would go down and see if they were visible. She would wait for Robert in the hall, she said, and she kissed us goodnight, and gave us her blessing.

What a dear she is! What a nice pet to leave us alone!

Robert and I passed another hour of bliss, and I think we must have got to the sixth heaven by now. Robert says the seventh is for the end, when we are married|well, that will be soon. Oh! I am too happy to write coherently.

I did not wake till late this morning, and Veronique came and said my sitting-room was again full of flowers. The darling Robert is!

I wrote to Christopher and Lady Ver, in bed as I sipped my chocolate. I just told Lady Ver the truth, that Robert and I had met by chance, and discovered we loved one another, so I knew she would understand|and I promised I would not break his heart. Then I thanked her for all her kindness to me, but I felt sad when I read it over|poor, dear Lady Ver|how I hope it won't really hurt her, and that she will forgive me.

To Christopher I said I had found my "variation" worth while, and I hoped he would come to my wedding some day soon.

Then I sent Veronique to post them both.

To-day I am moving to Carlton House Terrace. What a delight that will be|and in a fortnight, or at best three weeks, Robert says we shall quietly go and get married, and Colonel Tom Garden can give me away after all.

Oh the joy of the dear, beautiful world, and this sweet, dirty, enshrouding fog-bound London! I love it all|even the smuts!

18

SECTION 18

Carlton House Terrace,
Thursday night.

Robert came to see me at twelve, and he brought me the loveliest, splendid diamond and emerald ring, and I danced about like a child with delight over it. He has the most exquisite sentiment, Robert, every little trifle has some delicate meaning, and he makes me *fee I* and *feel.*

Each hour we spend together we seem to discover some new bit of us which is just what the other wants. And he is so deliciously jealous and masterful and|oh! I love him| so there it is!

I am learning a number of things, and I am sure there are lots to learn still.

At half past one Lady Merrenden came, and fetched us in the *barouche,* and off we went to Vavasour House, with what different feelings to last evening.

The pompous servants received us in state, and we all three walked on to the Duke's room.

There he was, still huddled in his chair, but he got up|he is better to-day.

Lady Merrenden went over and kissed him.

" Dear Torquilstone," she said.

" Morning, Robert," he mumbled, after he had greeted his aunt. " Introduce me to your *fianctt.* "

And Robert did with great ceremony.

" Now, I won't call you names any more," I said, and I laughed in his face. He bent down, and kissed my forehead.

" You are a beautiful tiger cat," he said, " but even a year of you would be well worth while."

Upon which Robert glared, and I laughed again, and we all went in to lunch.

He is not so bad, the Duke, after all!

Carlton House Terrace,

Dec. tut.

Oh ! it is three weeks since I wrote, but I have been too busy, and too happy, for journals. I have been here ever since, getting mytrousseau, and Veronique is becoming used to the fact that I can have no coronet on my *lingerie*!

It is the loveliest thing in the world being engaged to Robert!

He has ways !lWell, even if I really were as bad as I suppose I look, I could never want any one else. He worships me, and lets me order him about, and then he orders me about, and that makes me have the loveliest thrills! And if any one even looks at me in the street, which of course they always dolhe flashes blue fire at them, and I feelloh! I feel, all the time!

Lady Merrenden continues her sweet kindness to us, and her tact is beyond words, and now I often do what I used to wish tolthat is, touch Robert's eyelashes with the tips of my fingers!

It is perfectly lovely.

Oh, what in the world is the good of anything else in life, but being frantically in love like we are.

It all seems, to look back upon, as if it were like having porridge for breakfast, and nothing else every daylbefore I met Robert!

Perhaps it is because he is going to be very grand in the future, but every one has discovered I am a beauty, and intelligent. It is much nicer to be thought that than just to be a red-haired adventuress.

Lady Katherine, even, has sent me a cairngorm brooch and a cordial letter. (should now adorn her circle!)

But oh ! what do they all matterlwhat does anything matter but Robert! All day long I know I am learning the meaning of " to dance and to sing and to laugh and *to live.* "

The Duke and I are great friends, he has ferreted out about mamma's mother, and it appears she was a Venetian music mistress of the name of Tonquini, or something like that, who taught Lord de Brandreth's sisterslso perhaps Lady Ver was right after all, and far, far back in some other life, I was the friend of a Doge.

Poor dear Lady Ver! she has taken it very well after the first spiteful letter, and now I don't think there is even a tear at the corner of her eye!

Lady Merrenden says it is just the time of the year when she usually gets a new one, so perhaps she has now, and so that is all right.

The diamond serpent she has given me has emerald eyesland such a pointed tongue.

" It is like you, Snake-girl," she said, " so wear it at your wedding."

The three angels are to be my only bridesmaids.

Robert loads me with gifts, and the Duke is going to let me wear all the Torquilstone jewels when I am married, besides the emeralds he has given me himself. I really love him.

Christopher sent me this characteristic note with the earrings which are his gift, great big emeralds set with diamonds :

" So sorry I shall not see you on the happy day, but Paris, I am fortunate enough to discover, still has joys for me.

" C. C.

" Wear them, they will match your eyes ! "

19

SECTION 19

The Vicissitudes Of Evangeline

And to-morrow is my wedding-day, and I am going away on a honeymoon with Robert laway into the seventh heaven. And oh! and oh ! I am certain *sure* neither of us will yawn!

End Of Evangeline's Journal

CMISW1CK PKKSt: PRINTED BY CHARLES WH1TT1NGHAM AND CO. TOOKS COURT- CHANCBKV LANK, LONDON.

- '|$" " -
" ,

Lightning Source UK Ltd.
Milton Keynes UK
04 February 2010